I0450807

THE WELL AT THE
END OF THE WORLD
&
OTHER STORIES

Publications from
The Scheherazade Foundation

The Secrets of Scheherazade
An Ordered Experience
Tale of a Lantern & Other Stories
The Elephant & The Tortoise & Other Stories
The Monkey's Fiddle & Other Stories
Ghost of the Violet Well & Other Stories
Many Wise Fools & Other Stories
The Frog Prince & Other Stories
The Three Lemons & Other Stories
The Twelve-Headed Griffin & Other Stories
The Antelope Boy & Other Stories
Why the Fish Laughed & Other Stories
Two Cats & Other Stories
Three Stories
The Twilight of the Gods & Other Stories
The Son of Seven Queens & Other Stories
The Moon Maiden & Other Stories
The Metamorphosis & Other Stories
The Celestial Sisters & Other Stories
Tales from the Arabian Nights I
East of the Sun, West of the Moon & Other Stories
The Well at the End of the World & Other Stories

THE WELL AT THE END OF THE WORLD & OTHER STORIES

Edited & Introduced by

TAHIR SHAH

The Scheherazade Foundation

The Scheherazade Foundation CIC
85 Great Portland Street
London
W1W 7LT
United Kingdom
www.SF.Charity
info@SF.Charity

First published by The Scheherazade Foundation CIC, 2023

THE WELL AT THE END OF THE WORLD
&
OTHER STORIES

English Fairy Tales Flora Annie Steel Macmillan & Co. 1918	The Good Serpent *Journal of American Folklore* T. H. Moore 1894
The Prince's Elopement *Twenty-two Goblins* Arthur W. Ryder J.M. Dent Ltd. 1917	Seal Island *Ainu Folklore* Bronislas Pilsudski *Journal of American Folklore* 1912
Kanati & Selu: The Origin of Corn & Game *Myths of the Cherokees* James Mooney 1888	The Wicked Stepmother *The Journal of American Folklore* A. G. Seklimian 1897
The Tale of Suto & Tato *Bulletin of the School of Oriental Studies* Basile Nikitine & Major E. B. Soane 1923	Ricky of the Tuft *Folktexts: A Library of Folktales* D. L. Ashliman Dodd Mead & Co. 1921

Kanati & Selu: The Origin of Corn & Game
Myths of the Cherokee
James Mooney
Elder Booksellers Inc.
1900

The Children of the Sun
Aboriginal Myths & Traditions Concerning the Island of Titicaca
American Anthropologist
Adolph F. Bandelier
1904

The Fifty-one Thieves
Tagalog Folk-Tales
Journal of American Folklore
Fletcher Gardner
1907

The various authors listed above assert the right to be identified as the Authors of the Work in accordance with the Copyright, Designs and Patents Act 1988. A CIP catalogue record for this title is available from the British Library.

ISBN 978-1-915311-33-7

All rights reserved. No part of this publication may be reproduced, stored in a retrieval system, or transmitted, in any form or by any means, electronic, mechanical, photocopying, recording or otherwise, without the prior written permission of the publisher.

This book is sold subject to the condition that it shall not, by way of trade or otherwise, be lent, re-sold, hired out or otherwise circulated without the publisher's prior consent in any form of binding or cover other than that in which it is published and without a similar condition including this condition being imposed on the subsequent purchaser.

CONTENTS

Series Introduction

FROM EARLIEST CHILDHOOD, I was told stories.

Of course I was – most children are told stories.

After all, telling children stories is one of the foundations that makes their early experiences a childhood.

But as I think back to the first years of my own life, I find myself reeling from the sheer quantity of stories my infant ears took in.

Whereas other children my age were told stories for amusement, my parents (and the people they associated with) recounted the endless streams of tales for a different reason.

In their opinion, stories – and the ability to tell them – were part of an ancient alchemy... a way of processing complex ideas, of solving problems, and of developing the human mind.

My father, the writer and thinker Idries Shah, believed that folklore was the single most important breakthrough ever developed by the human species. The way he saw it, the rise of stories was as consequential as the development of the languages in which they were told.

He would say that, without stories and storytelling, humanity would never have evolved in the way that it has – and that the folktales, which form a bedrock of ancient societies, are more precious than any physical artefact unearthed on an archaeological dig.

As the years of my own childhood slipped by, I found myself unbothered to work out the hidden layers within treasuries of stories – what my father called 'instruction manuals to the world'. Like everyone else, I simply absorbed the individual tales, delighting in them.

And that's it – the key point, the genius of stories and storytelling.

It's a thing I only grasped in adulthood… something that fascinates me deeply.

In the same way you can jump into a car and drive across the country without giving a second thought to the engine or how it works, you can appreciate stories without understanding the hidden layers and devices that make them what they are.

Stories are all around us.

They're in the TV and movies we so adore, in the video games we play, and of course in the books we read. They're in newspapers and magazines, too; in the conversations we share with old friends, and with new ones. They're on our mobile phones, in aeroplanes, in submarines, and even in our dreams.

Our obsession with, and craving for, stories rests squarely with the way we are so absorbed by them, just as it does with the way we don't need to continually consider how and why they work.

Throughout my life, I've devoted an increasing amount of time to gathering stories from all corners of the world.

It began in my late teens, when I began to criss-cross the continents in a crazed preoccupation with folklore. I developed a first-hand love affair with societies that, over millennia, gave birth to their own astonishing traditions of stories and storytelling.

Most of the time, when reading or listening to stories, we forget that these tales have been shaped through the passage of time. Like pebbles in a river smoothed by rushing waters, they were honed through centuries of telling and retelling.

When I was twelve years old, my father published a masterwork, *World Tales*. The first edition was very large and featured hundreds of original illustrations. The book was unlike any that had come before, for it detailed the provenance and history of each story told.

At bedtime one night, he presented me with an advanced copy. For as long as I could remember, my father had been talking about the project.

Having an actual copy in my hands at last was thrilling beyond words.

Peering down at me sternly, my father said:

'This is far more than a book, Tahir Jan. It's the foundation stone of a great building… a building that *is* human culture. As you grow older, and as you go out into the world, you will understand that the folklores contained between the covers of *World Tales* have brought amusement and educated, and have solved problems when they were needed most of all.'

My father was right.

When I eventually headed out into the wilds of the world for the first time, I discovered the stories contained in *World Tales* for myself, along with a great many more. Just as he said, the stories published in his treasury were the warp and weft threads of society. Stories are the matrix on which culture itself is based – a framework that enables daily life to continue as smoothly as it does.

In this series of books, we have drawn together stories from all over the world. It's a mission begun decades ago by *World Tales*.

Some of the pieces will be known to you, and others will not.

Some will be easy to comprehend, while others will be challenging, or even nonsensical.

I'd now like to note something else…

The Occidental world seems to assume stories must appear in certain regimented ways – presented with a well-defined beginning, a middle, and an end. You know what I mean: the protagonist winning against all odds, and the happy ending to it all.

In the ancient tradition of teaching stories, the kind recounted for an eternity around campfires in the desert and in longhouses deep in the jungle, there's no such standardisation.

Rather, there's usually a hotchpotch of conflicting threads: stories without a straight linear narrative but with an underlying turbulence that gets the reader, or the listener, to sit up and think.

at The Scheherazade Foundation, we are preoccupied with the way we can extract knowledge from stories – either deliberately, or in a less structured way.

We hold the firm opinion that, in order to remove the marrow from the bone stories are best served up in the way as they were passed from one generation to the next throughout human history.

In this series, we have drawn together tales that were gathered in particular during the nineteenth and early twentieth centuries. Spanning a vast range of cultures, they offer an extraordinary glimpse into the societies from which they are drawn – societies that were often changed shortly afterwards by social upheaval, technologies, and war.

Indeed, the fact any of them were recorded at all is a thing of wonder.

Intriguingly, some of the tales will now appear dated because vocabulary and writing styles have altered. But the fact that they seem old-fashioned is of great interest – proof of the way stories are constantly changing and evolving from one era to the next.

Over the last thirty years, I've gathered hundreds of tales on my own journeys, most of them spoken directly into my ears by storytellers and fellow travellers, by wizened old men in the middle of nowhere, and by anyone else good enough to indulge my pleas.

On all those zigzagging adventures, one story sticks out, tantalising me whenever I turn it around my head.

It was called 'The Man Who Turned into a Cat'.

The reason I mention it here is not because it was an especially fine tale, but rather because, from that moment, it affected the way I perceive the world.

It was as though I were a lock and that, by hearing the tale, a key had been slipped into me and turned.

Since first receiving it, I've never been quite the same, my state of consciousness having been flipped inside out.

The fellow traveller who recounted 'The Man Who Turned into a Cat' was lost in shadow, no more than a fragment of his left cheek protruding shyly into the light.

We were sitting on low divans in a teahouse in the ancient Afghan city of Herat.

When the tale had been whispered, I sat there in silence for a long while.

'What have you done to me?' I asked after a long pause.

The fellow traveller offered half a smile.

'*I* didn't do anything,' he replied. 'It's the story that's affected you – a story that I myself first heard when I was a child playing in the orchards of Balkh.'

Peering into the shadow, my eyes widened.

'I don't understand,' I said feebly. 'After all, it's not an especially grand story. There wasn't even a jinn.'

The traveller's mouth eased out from the shadows.

Very slowly, it grinned.

'Tales containing the greatest sustenance for a soul speak in the softest voice,' he said.

Tahir Shah

The Well at the End of the World

ONCE UPON A time, and a very good time it was, though it wasn't in my time, nor in your time, nor anyone else's time, there was a girl whose mother had died, and her father had married again.

And her stepmother hated her because she was more beautiful than she was. And she was very cruel to her; she used to make her do all the servant's work, and never let her have any peace.

At last, one day, the stepmother thought to get rid of her altogether; so she handed her a sieve and said to her:

'Go, fill it at the Well at the End of the World and bring it home to me full, or woe betide you.'

For she thought she would never be able to find the Well of the World's End, and, if she did, how could she bring home a sieve full of water?

Well, the girl started off, and asked everyone she met to tell her where was the Well of the World's End. But nobody knew, and she didn't know what to do, when a queer little old woman, all bent double, told her where it was, and how she could get to it. So she did what the old woman told her, and at last arrived at the Well of the World's End.

But when she dipped the sieve in the cold, cold water, it all ran out again. She tried and she tried again, but every time it was the same; and at last she sat down and cried as if her heart would break.

Suddenly she heard a croaking voice, and she looked up and saw a great frog with goggle eyes looking at her and speaking to her.

'What's the matter, dearie?' it said.

'Oh dear! Oh dear!' she said, 'my stepmother has sent me all this long way to fill this sieve with water from the Well of the World's End, and I can't fill it no how at all.'

'Well,' said the frog, 'if you promise me to do whatever I bid you for a whole night long, I'll tell you how to fill it.'

So the girl agreed, and then the frog said:

'Stop it with moss and daub it with clay,

And then it will carry the water away'; and then it gave a hop, skip, and jump, and went flop into the Well of the World's End.

So the girl looked about for some moss, and lined the bottom of the sieve with it, and over that she put some clay, and then she dipped it once again into the Well of the World's End; and this time the water didn't run out, and she turned to go away.

Just then the frog popped up its head out of the Well of the World's End, and said, 'Remember your promise.'

'All right,' said the girl; for, thought she, 'what harm can a frog do me?'

So she went back to her stepmother, and brought the sieve full of water from the Well of the World's End. The stepmother was angry as angry, but she said nothing at all.

That very evening they heard something tap-tapping at the door low down, and a voice cried out:

'Open the door, my hinny, my heart,

Open the door, my own darling;

Remember the words that you and I spoke,

The Well at the End of the World but this morning.'

'Whatever can that be?' cried out the stepmother.

Then the girl had to tell her all about it, and what she had promised the frog.

'Girls must keep their promises,' said the stepmother, who was glad the girl would have to obey a nasty frog. 'Go and open the door this instant.'

So the girl went and opened the door, and there was the frog from the Well of the World's End. And it hopped, and it hopped, and it jumped, till it reached the girl, and then it said:

'Lift me up, my hinny, my heart,

Lift to your knee, my own darling;

Remember the words that you and I spoke,

The Well at the End of the World but this morning.'

But the girl would not do the frog's bidding, till her stepmother said, 'Lift it up this instant, you hussy! Girls *must* keep their promises!'

So she lifted the frog up on to her lap, and it lay there comfortably for a time; till at last it said:

'Give me some supper, my hinny, my heart,

Give me some supper, my darling;

Remember the words you and I spoke,

The Well at the End of the World but this morning.'

Well, that she did not mind doing, so she got it a bowl of milk and bread, and fed it well. But when the frog had finished, it said:

'Take me to bed, my hinny, my heart,

Take me to bed, my own darling;

Remember the promise you promised to me,

The Well at the End of the World but this morning.'

But that the girl refused to do, till her stepmother said harshly:

'Do what you promised, girl; girls *must* keep their promises. Do what you're bid, or out you go, you and your froggie.'

So the girl took the frog with her to bed, and kept it as far away from her as she could. Well, just as the day was beginning to break, what should the frog say but:

'Chop off my head, my hinny, my heart,

Chop off my head, my own darling;

Remember the promise you promised to me,

The Well at the End of the World but this morning.'

At first the girl wouldn't, for she thought of what the frog had done for her at the Well of the World's End. But when the frog said the words over and over again in a pleading voice, she went and took an axe and chopped off its head, and, lo and behold! There stood before her a handsome young prince, who told her that he had been enchanted by a wicked magician, and he could never be unspelled till some girl would do his bidding for a whole night, and chop off his head at the end of it.

The stepmother was surprised indeed when she found the young prince instead of the nasty frog, and she was not best pleased, you may be sure, when the prince told her that he was going to marry her stepdaughter because she had unspelled him.

But married they were, and went away to live in the castle of the king, his father; and all the stepmother had to console her was, that it was all through *her* that her stepdaughter was married to a prince.

From: English Fairy Tales

The Good Serpent

THOU MUST KNOW to tell, and understand in order to know that there was a gentleman who had three children; two sons, and a daughter whose name was 'Mariquita'. This one was precisely the darling of her father and brothers.

One day when she was in the garden she found a little snake; she took it up and put it in her bosom. There she nursed it, and when it was bigger she kept it inside a trunk. Every day she kept a plate of food, went to the trunk, opened it, and said to the snake, 'Sister mine, Florita!'

The snake answered, 'What wantest thou, sweetheart?' put out its head and ate the food. Her father noticed this. For whom should she hide away food? And set his servants to spy upon her. When they saw the serpent, that had grown ever so big, they were very frightened, and went running to the master to tell him that the food was for a very horrid animal.

The gentleman went to see it, and indeed the sight of the serpent put one in a fright; he ordered a servant to go with it to a wooded height and to kill it. In vain the maiden begged him to leave it with her, since she had brought it up from a very little one, but her father was not willing, only he told the servant instead of killing it, to cast it alive into the wood.

The maiden remained weeping very much for her snake, for she liked it as if it were a sister; so she passed many days very sorrowful.

One day her father had to send his two sons with a message to the king, who lived in a neighbouring town. Being one day at the king's table, they were relating many things to him (for they were very well instructed in everything), and amongst others they said to him,

'We have a very singular sister, for when she laughs she lets fall fine pearls; when she washes her hands, the water next day changes into a block of silver; and when she combs her hair, the hair that falls off becomes golden threads.'

'Is this possible?' said the king.

'So possible is it,' said the young men, 'that we will lose our heads if it be not as we have said.'

'Very well,' said the king, 'I am going to ask for your sister in marriage, and if what you have told me does not turn out true, I will order your heads to be cut off, as a punishment for having deceived me.'

Soon after he sent messengers to their father, asking him for Mariquita, to become the king's wife. Now, besides the gifts which her brothers had talked of, she was beautiful as the sun, and good.

Her father consented, highly pleased; and sent her to the king, accompanied by her nurse. The latter had a daughter named Estefania, and she and her daughter were very bad-hearted and envious. When they had travelled halfway, Mariquita fell asleep; so Estefania said to her mother, 'Can you tell what I am thinking about?'

'What is it?' said she to her.

'That it would be a good thing if we were to put out Mariquita's eyes, and cast her off in this wooded height (now just then they were passing through a thickly wooded spot), and as the king does not know which is Mariquita, we will tell him that I am she, and I shall be married to him.'

'Very well,' said the old woman to her; so they did so, but seeing that the eyes were very beautiful, they put them in a glass to keep them.

The maiden passed a dreadful night in the wood, for that night it rained and thundered a great deal; she was half dead with pain and cold. The following day there came a little old man to the wood with his little donkey, to get a load of firewood to take to sell in the town, and with the money to buy a bag of bran for his family, for he could not do any better for them. Instead of getting firewood he found the maiden, and moved by pity he took her to his house on his little donkey. The little old man had three bad-hearted daughters, who treated him very badly.

When they saw him coming without firewood and a woman in its stead they began to cry out,

'Bad old man, what wilt thou give us to eat today? It will be this woman mayhap? She is coming to bring another mouth to the house that we may come to an end once for all by dying of hunger! Of what use is this blind wench who cannot gain her living?'

The little old man said to them,

'Have patience, daughters; this poor creature was in the wood, and I have brought her out of pity. I am going quickly for the load of firewood, and you shall soon have your dinners. I will leave my share and will give it to her.'

But his daughters scolded him more and more, for that blind wench he would die of want, and then who was going to work for them? At last he managed to pacify them a little, went for the firewood, sold it, and brought them their food.

Meanwhile the daughters ill-treated Mariquita in all sorts of ways, until at last one of them more merciful than the others got them to leave her in peace.

The maiden said to this one,

'Little sister, bring me a little water to wash my hands.'

She brought it to her in a broken earthen pot.

But the others cried out,

'What a fine lady! She does not like to go and wash herself in the river!'

But the kind one said,

'There now, don't you see that the poor little thing is blind, and might fall into the water?'

She washed her hands, and said,

'Keep this water, little sister, till tomorrow.'

The old man's daughter said,

'But tomorrow I will bring thee fresh water.'

Mariquita said, 'But I want the same.'

At last the girl put it away among some shrubs, spilling a little on the ground.

The next day Mariquita said,

'Little sister, bring me the water that I asked thee yesterday to keep for me.'

She went to bring it, and found in its stead a block of silver, and silver on the ground where the water was spilt; and in bringing it the potsherd came to pieces from the weight of the silver.

'What is this,' said she, 'that I have found instead of the water?'

Mariquita said,

'This is silver; tell Daddy to go to the town and sell it, for it is worth a great deal, and let him buy for you clothes and food.'

The little old man did as Mariquita said; they bought it of him for a great deal of money; he bought plenty of clothes and plenty of food, and went home well pleased, for he had never even dreamed of so much riches.

Mariquita laughed heartily at the surprise of these people; and while she laughed, gathered in her lap the pearls that fell from her mouth. Then she said to the little old man,

'Take these, Daddy, they are fine pearls; take them to the town and sell them, for they are worth a great deal. Buy more food and all that you need.'

Meanwhile she asked the girls for a comb, to comb her hair. They brought her one; for since she had made them rich, they were so kind to her that they did not know what to make of her. She began to comb herself at the corner of the fireplace; and the girls to take care of her feet that she might warm them, put them so close to the fire that it almost burnt them.

She kept the hair that fell from her head, and the next day she had a handful of golden threads.

'Take these, Daddy,' said she to the little old man, 'and go to town and sell them, for they are threads of gold. Buy all you need; all that you get for them is for you.'

The little old man was well pleased, and brought much money to his daughters.

Meanwhile, Estefania had arrived at the king's palace. He received her with great kindness, and married her on the spot.

On the morrow he made her wash her hands, and put away the water, but the next day it was nothing but water. He made her laugh, but not a single pearl fell from her mouth. He made her comb herself, and kept the fallen hair, but hair it was, and hair it remained. So he slapped his forehead, and said,

'These young men have deceived me; I will order their heads to be cut off!'

He did so, and had their bodies embalmed to be sent to their father. Estefania went on living with the king, and the time was drawing nigh that she was about to have a baby, so that she was full of longings for everything she set eyes on.

One day that Mariquita was sitting in the sun, at the door of the little old man's hut, his daughters saw a big serpent that went towards Mariquita.

'Ay!' they said, 'come away from there! There is a big serpent, a very dreadful one, that is going to eat thee!'

She said to them,

'He will not hurt me, only let him come!'

The girls wanted to kill it, but Mariquita would not let them. The serpent came near to her, caressed her a great deal, and began to lick the sockets of her eyes, for it was the same which she had reared from a little snake.

It said to Mariquita, 'Thy foster sister Estefania will soon have a baby, and all that she sets eyes on she longs for. Send the little old man to the town, let him buy the most beautiful nosegay of flowers that he can find, and take it to sell at the king's palace.'

The little old man did so, and when he passed by the palace, cried out,

'Who buys nosegays?'

Estefania said to her mother,

'I must have that nosegay!'

Her mother asked the little old man what it was worth, and he told her that he sold it for eyes.

'Mother,' said Estefania, 'let us take out the eyes of the dog and give them to him.'

The old man took them and went his way; but, before he got home with them the serpent said,

'Eyes are coming, Mariquita, but they are not thine, thine will come later.'

When the little old man arrived, the serpent said to him,

'Throw them away, Daddy, they are dog's eyes!'

The next day Mariquita told him to buy another nosegay finer still, and pass by the palace to sell it for eyes. Estefania came out, as on the day before, to buy it, and said to her mother,

'Let us take out the cat's eyes, and give them to him.'

They did so, and the little old man took them, but before he came home the serpent said,

'Eyes are coming, Mariquita, but they are not thine, thine will come later.'

So she said to the little old man,

'Throw them away, Daddy, they are cat's eyes.'

The following day, they sent to buy a nosegay more beautiful than the others, with birds singing on the top of it, and the little old man went to the palace to sell it.

Estefania came out to buy it, and said to her mother,

'Now we have no more eyes, what shall we do, for I must have the nosegay?'

Her mother said to her,

'Dost thou not remember that we kept Mariquita's eyes in a glass; we will see if they are sweet yet.'

Estefania said,

'So long ago, they must be rotten.'

They went to look for them, and found them the same as when they had taken them out, so they gave them to him for the nosegay. Before the little old man got home, the serpent said,

'Eyes are coming, Mariquita, and they are thine!'

So when he arrived she was well pleased, and said,

'These, Daddy, are really my eyes.'

She took them and gave them to the serpent. The serpent licked the sockets, put the eyes in again, and if beautiful they were before, much more beautiful were they afterwards.

The next day the serpent said,

'Let us go to the palace. Take this bag of gold ounces, and as the king takes his afternoon nap with Estefania, and has his guards at the door, thou must throw a handful of ounces to the soldiers, and while they are busy in gathering them up, thou must cry at the door, 'Sister mine, Florita!'

I will answer, 'What wilt thou, sweetheart?'

Thou wilt say –

'My servant Estefania
In the king's arms asleep;
Woe is me because of a faithless wretch.

19

Thou wilt fling another handful of ounces to the guards, and while they pick them up we will escape.'

They did so one day, but the king, who had seen and heard all, gave orders to his guards to seize Mariquita and the serpent when they came again. But the guards, busied with picking up the ounces, took no notice of the king's orders. The third day, the king himself got behind the door to seize them, since he could not get his guards to do it, even though he threatened to cut their heads off. When they came the third time, and said the same things, and were running away, the king took hold of Mariquita by her clothes and stopped her.

'What is this, maiden,' said he, 'what wert thou saying?'

Therewith the serpent spoke up for her and said,

'It is that the wife that your royal majesty has is not Mariquita. She is here; order her to do the wonders which her brothers spoke of.'

She then told all that the two wicked women had done with Mariquita on the way to the palace.

The king, very wroth, took her indoors, made her wash her hands, kept the water, and the next day it had changed into a block of silver. He made her comb her hair, and the hair that fell off became golden threads. She laughed and fine pearls fell from her mouth.

The king acknowledged his mistake, and felt very sorry for having killed so unjustly the brothers; he married Mariquita, and ordained great royal feasts, and ordered Estefania and her mother to be broken on the wheel, quartered, afterwards to be burnt and their ashes cast to the winds.

After some time had passed, Mariquita had twin princes. Once when they were lying in the cradle, and their parents fondling them, the serpent came, and said,

'Which should you like best; to see, your sons dead, or your brothers alive?'

They answered,

'Our sons dead, since they are angels from heaven, and our brothers alive.'

The serpent cut the infants' throats, and led the parents to the place where the bodies of the two brothers lay embalmed, and they found them alive and well. The parents then felt very sorrowful, and went back to weep over their children; when they found them alive, and playing in the cradle.

The serpent said to them,

'I have now done all that I can do for you. I have no more business here, for I am an angel sent by God, and I am going back to heaven. Farewell.'

The tale is finished.

From: Journal of American Folklore

The Prince's Elopement

ON THE BANK of the Godavari River is a kingdom called the Abiding Kingdom. There lived the son of King Victory, the famous King Triple-victory, mighty as the king of the gods. As this king sat in judgment, a monk called 'Patience' brought him every day one piece of fruit as an expression of homage. And the king took it and gave it each day to the treasurer who stood near.

Thus twelve years passed.

Now one day the monk came to court, gave the king a piece of fruit as usual, and went away. But on this day the king gave the fruit to a pet baby monkey that had escaped from his keepers, and happened to wander in. And as the monkey ate the fruit, he split it open, and a priceless, magnificent gem came out.

When the king saw this, he took it and asked the treasurer,

'Where have you been keeping the fruits which the monk brought? I gave them to you.'

On hearing this, the treasurer was frightened. He said,

'Your Majesty, I have thrown them all through the window. If your Majesty desires, I will look for them now.'

And when the king had dismissed him, he went, but returned in a moment, and said again,

'Your Majesty, they were all smashed in the treasury, and in them I see heaps of dazzling gems.'

When he heard this, the king was delighted, and gave the jewels to the treasurer. And when the monk came the next day, he asked him,

'Monk, why do you keep honouring me in such an expensive way? Unless I know the reason, I will not take your fruit.'

Then the monk took the king aside and said,

'O hero, there is a business in which I need help. So I ask for your help in it, because you are a brave man.'

And the king promised his assistance. Then the monk was pleased, and said again,

'O King, on the last night of the waning moon, you must go to the great cemetery at nightfall, and come to me under the fig tree.'

Then the king said,

'Certainly,' and Patience, the monk, went home well pleased.

So when the night came, the mighty king remembered his promise to the monk, and at dusk he wrapped his head in a black veil, took his sword in his hand, and went to the great cemetery without being seen.

When he got there, he looked about, and saw the monk standing under the fig tree and making a magic circle.

So he went up and said,

'Monk, here I am. Tell me what I am to do for you.'

And when the monk saw the king, he was delighted and said,

'O King, if you wish to do me a favour, go south from here some distance all alone, and you will see a sissoo tree and a dead body hanging from it. Be so kind as to bring that here.'

When the brave king heard this, he agreed, and, true to his promise, turned south and started. And as he walked with difficulty along the cemetery road, he came upon the sissoo tree at some distance, and saw a body hanging on it. So he climbed the tree, cut the rope, and let it fall to the ground.

And as it fell, it unexpectedly cried aloud, as if alive.

Then the king climbed down, and thinking it was alive, he mercifully rubbed its limbs. Then the body gave a loud laugh.

So the king knew that a goblin lived in it, and said without fear,

'What are you laughing about? Come, let us be off.'

But then he did not see the goblin on the ground any longer. And when he looked up, there he was, hanging in the tree as before. So the king climbed the tree again, and carefully carried the body down. A brave man's heart is harder than a diamond, and nothing makes it tremble.

Then he put the body with the goblin in it on his shoulder, and started off in silence. And as he walked along, the goblin in the body said,

'O King, to amuse the journey, I will tell you a story. Listen.'

There is a city called Benares where Shiva lives. It is loved by pious people like the soil of Mount Kailasa.

The river of heaven shines there like a pearl necklace.

And in the city lived a king called Valour who burned up all his enemies by his valour, as a fire burns a forest. He had a son named Thunderbolt who broke the pride of the love god by his beauty, and the pride of men by his bravery. This prince had a clever friend, the son of a counsellor.

One day the prince was enjoying himself with his friend hunting, and went a long distance. And so he came to a great forest. There he saw a beautiful lake, and being tired, he drank from it with his friend the counsellor's son, washed his hands and feet, and sat down under a tree on the bank.

And then he saw a beautiful maiden who had come there with her servants to bathe. She seemed to fill the lake with the stream of her beauty, and seemed to make lilies grow there with her eyes, and seemed to shame the lotuses with a face more lovely than the moon. She captured the prince's heart the moment that he saw her. And the prince took her eyes captive.

The girl had a strange feeling when she saw him, but was too modest to say a word. So she gave a hint of the feeling in her heart. She put a lotus on her ear, laid a lily on her head after she had made the edge look like a row of teeth, and placed her hand on her heart. But the prince did not understand her signs, only the clever counsellor's son understood them all.

A moment later the girl went away, led by her servants.

She went home and sat on the sofa and stayed there. But her thoughts were with the prince.

The prince went slowly back to his city, and was terribly lonely without her, and grew thinner every day. Then his friend the son of the counsellor took him aside and told him that she was not hard to find. But he had lost all courage and said,

'My friend, I don't know her name, nor her home, nor her family. How can I find her? Why do you vainly try to comfort me?'

Then the counsellor's son said,

'Did you not see all that she hinted with her signs? When she put the lotus on her ear, she meant that she lived in the kingdom of a king named Ear-lotus. And when she made the row of teeth, she meant that she was the daughter of a man named Bite there.

'And when she laid the lily on her head, she meant that her name was Lily. And when she placed her hand on her heart, she meant that she loved you. And there is a king named Ear-lotus in the Kalinga country.

'There is a very rich man there whom the king likes. His real name is Battler, but they call him Bite. He has a pearl of a girl whom he loves more than his life, and her name is Lily. This is true, because people told me. So I understood her signs about her country and the other things.'

When the counsellor's son had said this, the prince was delighted to find him so clever, and pleased because he knew what to do.

Then he formed a plan with the counsellor's son, and started for the lake again, pretending that he was going to hunt, but really to find the girl that he loved. On the way he rode like the wind away from his soldiers, and started for the Kalinga country with the counsellor's son.

When they reached the city of King Ear-lotus, they looked about and found the house of the man called Bite, and they went to a house nearby to live with an old woman. And the counsellor's son said to the old woman,

'Old woman, do you know anybody named Bite in this city?'

Then the old woman answered him respectfully,

'My son, I know him well. I was his nurse. And I am a servant of his daughter Lily. But I do not go there now because my dress is stolen. My naughty son is a gambler and steals my clothes.'

Then the counsellor's son was pleased and satisfied her with his own cloak and other presents. And he said,

'Mother, you must do very secretly what we tell you. Go to Bite's daughter Lily, and tell her that the prince whom she saw on the bank of the lake is here, and sent you with a love message to her.'

The old woman was pleased with the gifts and went to Lily at once. And when she got a chance, she said,

'My child, the prince and the counsellor's son have come to take you. Tell me what to do now.'

But the girl scolded her and struck her cheeks with both hands smeared with camphor.

The old woman was hurt by this treatment, and came home weeping, and said to the two men,

'My sons, see how she left the marks of her fingers on my face.'

And the prince was hopeless and sad, but the very clever counsellor's son took him aside and said,

'My friend, do not be sad. She was only keeping the secret when she scolded the old woman, and put ten fingers white with camphor on her face. She meant that you must wait before seeing her, for the next ten nights are bright with moonlight.'

So the counsellor's son comforted the prince, took a little gold ornament and sold it in the market, and bought a great dinner for the old woman. So they two took dinner with the old woman. They did this for ten days, and then the counsellor's son sent her to Lily again, to find out something more.

And the old woman was eager for dainty food and drink. So to please him she went to Lily's house, and then came back and said,

'My children, I went there and stayed with her for some time without speaking. But she spoke herself of my naughtiness in mentioning you, and struck me again on the chest with three fingers stained red. So I came back in disgrace.'

Then the counsellor's son whispered to the prince,

'Don't be alarmed, my friend. When she left the marks of three red fingers on the old woman's heart, she meant to say very cleverly that there were three dangerous days coming.'

So the counsellor's son comforted the prince.

And when three days were gone, he sent the old woman to Lily again. And this time she went and was very respectfully entertained, and treated to wine and other things the whole day. But when she was ready to go back in the evening, a terrible shouting was heard outside. They heard people running and crying,

'Oh, oh! A mad elephant has escaped from his stable and is running around and stamping on people.'

Then Lily said to the old woman,

'Mother, you must not go through the street now where the elephant is. I will put you in a swing and let you down with ropes through this great window into the garden. Then you can climb into a tree and jump on the wall, and go home by way of another tree.'

So she had her servants let the old woman down from the window into the garden by a rope swing. And the old woman went home and told the prince and the counsellor's son all about it.

Then the counsellor's son said to the prince,

'My friend, your wishes are fulfilled. She has been clever enough to show you the road. So you must follow that same road this very evening to the room of your darling.'

So the prince went to the garden with the counsellor's son by the road that the old woman had shown them. And there he saw the rope swing hanging down, and servants above keeping an eye on the road. And when he got into the swing, the servants at the window pulled at the rope and he came to his darling.

And when he had gone in, the counsellor's son went back to the old woman's house.

But the prince saw Lily, and her face was beautiful like the full moon, and the moonlight of her beauty shone forth, like the night when the moon shines in secret because of the dark. And when she saw him, she threw her arms around his neck and kissed him. So he married her and stayed hidden with her for some days.

One day he said to his wife,

'My dear, my friend the counsellor's son came with me, and he is staying all alone at the old woman's house. I must go and see him, then I will come back.'

But Lily was shrewd and said,

'My dear, I must ask you something. Did you understand the signs I made, or was it the counsellor's son?'

And the prince said to her,

'My dear, I did not understand them all, but my friend has wonderful wisdom. He understood everything and told me.'

Then the sweet girl thought, and said,

'My dear, you did wrong not to tell me before. Your friend is a real brother to me. I ought to have sent him some nuts and other nice things at the very first.'

Then she let him go, and he went to his friend by night by the same road, and told all that his wife had said. But the counsellor's son said,

'That is foolish,' and did not think much of it.

So they spent the night talking.

Then when the time for the twilight sacrifice came, a friend of Lily's came there with cooked rice and nuts in her hand. She came and asked the counsellor's son about his health and gave him the present. And she cleverly tried to keep the prince from eating.

'Your wife is expecting you to dinner,' she said, and a moment later she went away.

Then the counsellor's son said to the prince,

'Look, your Majesty. I will show you something curious.'

So he took a little of the cooked rice and gave it to a dog that was there. And the moment he ate it, the dog died. And the prince asked the counsellor's son what this strange thing could mean.

And he replied,

'Your Majesty, she knew that I was clever because I understood her signs, and she wanted to kill me out of love for you. For she thought the prince would not be all her own while I was alive, but would leave her for my sake and go back to his own city. So she sent me poisoned food to eat. But you must not be angry with her. I will think up some scheme.'

Then the prince praised the counsellor's son, and said,

'You are truly the body of wisdom.'

And then suddenly a great wailing of grief-stricken people was heard,

'Alas! Alas! The king's little son is dead.'

When he heard this, the counsellor's son was delighted, and said,

'Your Majesty, go tonight to Lily's house, and make her drink wine until she loses her senses and seems to be dead. Then as she lies there, make a mark on her hip with a red-hot fork, steal her jewels, and come back the old way through the window. After that I will do the right thing.'

Then he made a three-pronged fork and gave it to the prince. And the prince took the crooked, cruel thing, hard as the weapon of Death, and went by night as before to Lily's house.

'A king,' he thought, 'ought not to disregard the words of a high-minded counsellor.'

So when he had stupefied her with wine, he branded her hip with the fork, stole her jewels, returned to his friend, and told him everything, showing him the jewels.

Then the counsellor's son felt sure his scheme was successful. He went to the cemetery in the morning, and disguised himself as a hermit, and the prince as his pupil.

And he said, 'Take this pearl necklace from among the jewels. Go and sell it in the marketplace. And if the policemen arrest you, say this: It was given to me to sell by my teacher.'

So the prince went to the marketplace and stood there offering the pearl necklace for sale, and he was arrested while doing it by the policemen. And as they were eager to find out about the theft of the jewels from Bite's daughter, they took the prince at once to the chief of police. And when he saw that the culprit was dressed like a hermit, he asked him very gently,

'Holy sir, where did you get this pearl necklace? It belongs to Bite's daughter and was stolen.'

Then the prince said to them,

'Gentlemen, my teacher gave it to me to sell. You had better go and ask him.'

Then the chief of police went and asked him,

'Holy sir, how did this pearl necklace come into your pupil's hand?'

And the shrewd counsellor's son whispered to him,

'Sir, as I am a hermit, I wander about all the time in this region. And as I happened to be here in this cemetery, I saw a whole company of witches who came here at night. And one of the witches split open the heart of a king's son, and offered it to her master. She was mad with wine, and screwed up her face most horribly.

But when she impudently tried to snatch my rosary as I prayed, I became angry, and branded her on the hip with a three-pronged fork which I had made red-hot with a magic spell. And I took this pearl necklace from her neck. Then, as it was not a thing for a hermit, I sent it to be sold.'

When he heard this, the chief of police went and told the whole story to the king. And when the king heard and saw the evidence, he sent the old woman, who was reliable, to identify the pearl necklace. And he heard from her that Lily was branded on the hip.

Then he was convinced that she was really a witch and had devoured his son. So he went himself to the counsellor's son, who was disguised as a hermit, and asked how Lily should be punished. And by his advice, she was banished from the city, though her parents wept. So she was banished naked to the forest and knew that the counsellor's son had done it all, but she did not die.

And at nightfall the prince and the counsellor's son put off their hermit disguise, mounted on horseback, and found her weeping. They put her on a horse and took her to their own country. And when they got there, the prince lived most happily with her.

But Bite thought that his daughter was eaten by wild beasts in the wood, and he died of grief. And his wife died with him.

When he had told this story, the goblin asked the king,

'O King, who was to blame for the death of the parents: the prince, or the counsellor's son, or Lily? You seem like a very wise man, so resolve my doubts on this point. If you know and do not tell me the truth, then your head will surely fly into a hundred pieces. And if you give a good answer, then I will jump from your shoulder and go back to the sissoo tree.'

Then King Triple-victory said to the goblin,

'You are a master of magic. You surely know yourself, but I will tell you. It was not the fault of any of the three you mentioned. It was entirely the fault of King Ear-lotus.'

But the goblin said,

'How could it be the king's fault? The other three did it. Are the crows to blame when the geese eat up the rice?'

Then the king said,

'But those three are not to blame. It was right for the counsellor's son to do his master's business. So he is not to blame. And Lily and the prince were madly in love and could not stop to think. They only looked after their own affairs. They are not to blame.

'But the king knew the law books very well, and he had spies to find out the facts among the people. And he knew about the doings of rascals. So he acted without thinking. He is to blame.'

When the goblin heard this, he wanted to test the king's constancy.

So he went back by magic in a moment to the sissoo tree.

And the king went back fearlessly to get him.

From: Twenty-Two Goblins

Seal Island

My GRANDFATHER HAD brought me up, feeding me on the flesh of sea animals which he brought home. Thus we lived. One year, as usual, my grandfather went out to sea to kill some animals, that I might have something to eat.

When he came home, late in the afternoon, he had killed no game.

Then he said to me,

'I have been on the island where I go every year to get game for our living, but there was not one seal on the island. I heard their roaring, though, far out at sea – the roaring of old beasts. So I thought that the old seals had wandered away from our island to another place. It is a long time since the island that has fed us for so long has been crowded with seals. Now there is not one animal left there; so I came back without killing anything.'

This is what my grandfather said.

From the moment I heard his words, I kept thinking how I might reach this far-off island. The thought kept me awake nights.

One night, when my grandfather was sound asleep, I went down to the seashore. There I took the boat which my grandfather used for hunting, pulled it out on the water, and steered in the direction of the other sea.

Rowing with all my strength, I soon came in sight of an island far out at sea. A few more strokes of the oars brought me quite close to it, and at last I was able to land.

There were lots of seals everywhere.

But from the end of the island a miserable little man appeared. He approached, and soon began to scold me.

'Why did you come? Why did you come out on this island?

The creatures here are much worse than elsewhere, so why did you come? It is very dangerous to stay here. Hide your boat in yonder cave in the rock, fill it with killed seals, and secret yourself among their bodies. The awful god of the island is near, so you must hide before he sees you.'

The god then arrived; and I heard him ask,

'What is this boat?'

And Self-brought-up-Man answered,

'It is my boat.'

'But the little sitting board is fastened to it with a rope which was twisted with the left hand, and it smells like the smell of a human being,' said the evil god again.

'I am only half god and half man,' Self-brought-up-Man answered, 'so the boat may be human, and its smell is human.'

'Self-brought-up-Man,' said the god, 'you are mighty and fearless, and so are your deeds; but today we shall measure our powers.'

This is what he said, and I heard it.

Then the evil god went home; and Self-brought-up-Man turned towards me, and said,

'My child, go back to your village as quickly as you can; and when you are sailing near the head of the island, carve an 'inau' out of a birch tree, and one out of an ash tree, and put them into your boat. Carve out an 'inau' from the 'uita' tree, which is the tree of the evil god, and leave it on the island. Your father was a great friend of mine in my youth, therefore I warn you not to come here again, because this land is very dangerous. When you have gone, and are in the middle of the sea, you will hear the din and roar of the battle between the god and myself, and a bloody rain will fall on your boat from above. This will be a sign that I am hurt. But you will go farther still, and again a bloody rain will fall (at the rear of your boat this time), and you will look back and see me kill that evil god. As long as you are away from home, your grandfather will be uneasy about you. He is walking to and fro on the path on which you went away, to the end of it, leaning on a big stick. He knows that you are on this island, and he is praying to me to help you. His words strike the clouds, and his prayers fall on my head from above. Direct your boat under that rainbow!'

On looking up, I saw that I was near my home, and my grandfather was walking on the sand of the shore, leaning on a thick stick. He was looking so hard up at the sky, and was praying so fervently, that he never noticed me, though I landed just in front of him.

I took two seals out of the boat, one in each hand, carried them to my grandfather, and threw them down in front of him. He was so frightened that he fell down on his back.

Then only did he look at me, and he was very glad to see me. He patted me on the back and on the chest, and began to scold me gently.

'What have you been doing? Why did you go to that island? If it had not been for my friend, Self-brought-up-Man, I should see your body no more.'

So I went home, skinned the dead animals, cut out quantities of meat, cooked it, and gave my grandfather to eat. After a time my grandfather said to me,

'I am old, and my death is near. After I am dead, do not go to the island whence you have just come, because it is dangerous for you.'

From: Ainu Folklore

Kanati & Selu: The Origin of Corn & Game

WHEN I WAS a boy, this is what the old men told me they had heard when they were boys. Long ages ago, soon after the world was made, a hunter and his wife lived at Looking-glass Mountain, with their only child, a little boy.

The father's name was Kanati, 'The Lucky Hunter,' and his wife was called Selu, which means 'corn'.

No matter when Kanati went into the woods, he never failed to bring back a load of game, which his wife cut up and prepared, washing the blood from the meat in the river near the house. The little boy used to play down by the river every day, and one morning the old people thought they heard laughing and talking in the bushes, as though there were two children there.

When the boy came home at night, his parents asked who had been playing with him all day.

'He comes out of the water,' said the boy, and he calls himself my elder brother. He says his mother was cruel to him, and threw him into the river.'

Then they knew that the strange boy had sprung from the blood of the game which Selu had washed off at the river's edge.

Every day, when the little boy went out to play, the other would join him; but, as he always went back into the water, the old people never had a chance to see him. At last, one evening, Kanati said to his son,

'Tomorrow, when the other boy comes to play with you, get him to wrestle with you, and when you have your arms around him hold on to him and call for us.'

The boy promised to do as he was told; so the next day, as soon as his playmate appeared, he challenged him to a wrestling match. The other agreed at once, but as soon as they had their arms around each other Kanati's boy began to scream for his father. The old folks at once came running down, and when the wild boy saw them he struggled to free himself, and cried out,

'Let me go! You threw me away!'

But his brother held on until his parents reached the spot, when they seized the wild boy and took him home with them. They kept him in the house until they had tamed him, but he was always wild and artful in his disposition, and was the leader of his brother in every mischief. Before long the old people discovered that he was one of those persons endowed with magic powers, and they called him,

'He who grew up Wild.'

Whenever Kanati went into the mountains be always brought back a fat buck or doe, or may be a couple of turkeys. One day the wild boy said to his brother,

'I wonder where our father gets all that game; let's follow him next time, and find out.'

A few days afterward, Kanati took a bow and some feathers in his hand, and started off.

The boys waited a little while, and then started after him, keeping out of sight, until they saw their father go into a swamp where there were a great many of the reeds that hunters use to make arrow-shafts. Then the wild boy changed himself into a puff of bird's down, which the wind took up and carried until it alighted upon Kanati's shoulder just as he entered the swamp, but Kanati knew nothing about it. The hunter then cut reeds, fitted the feathers to them, and made some arrows, and the wild boy – in his other shape – thought:

'I wonder what those things are for.'

When Kanati had his arrows finished, he came out of the swamp and went on again. The wind blew the down from his shoulder; it fell in the woods, when the wild boy took his right shape again, and went back and told his brother what he had seen.

Keeping out of sight of their father, they followed him up the mountain until he stopped at a certain place and lifted up a large rock. At once a buck came running out, which Kanati shot, and then, lifting it upon his back, he started home again.

'Oho!' said the boys, 'he keeps all the deer shut up in that hole, and whenever he wants venison he just lets one out, and kills it with those things he made in the swamp.'

They hurried and reached home before their father, who had the heavy deer to carry, so that he did not know they had followed him.

A few days after, the boys went back to the swamp, cut some reeds and made seven arrows, and then started up the mountain to where their father kept the game.

When they got to the place they lifted up the rock, and a deer came running out. Just as they drew back to shoot it, another came out, and then another, and another, until the boys got confused and forgot what they were about.

In those days all the deer had their tails hanging down, like other animals, but, as a buck was running past, the wild boy struck its tail with his arrow so that it stood straight out behind. This pleased the boys, and when the next one ran by, the other brother struck his tail so that it pointed upward.

The boys thought this was good sport, and when the next one ran past, the wild boy struck his tail so that it stood straight up, and his brother struck the next one so hard with his arrow that the deer's tail was curled over his back. The boys thought this was very pretty, and ever since the deer has carried his tail over his back.

The deer continued to pass until the last one had come out of the hole and escaped into the forest. Then followed droves of raccoons, rabbits, and all the other four-footed animals. Last came great flocks of turkeys, pigeons, and partridges that darkened the air like a cloud, and made such a noise with their wings that Kanati, sitting at home, heard the sound like distant thunder on the mountains, and said to himself,

'My bad boys have got into trouble. I must go and see what they are doing.'

So Kanati went up the mountain, and when he came to the place where he kept the game he found the two boys standing by the rock, and all the birds and animals were gone. He was furious, but, without saying a word, he went down into the cave and kicked the covers off four jars in one corner, when out swarmed bed bugs, fleas, lice, and gnats, and got all over the boys.

They screamed with pain and terror, and tried to beat off the insects; but the thousands of insects crawled over them, and bit and stung them, until both dropped down nearly dead from exhaustion. Kanati stood looking on until he thought they had been punished enough, when he brushed off the vermin, and proceeded to give the boys a lecture.

'Now, you rascals,' said he, 'you have always had plenty to eat, and never had to work for it. Whenever you were hungry, all I had to do was to come up here and get a deer or a turkey, and bring it home for your mother to cook. But now you have let out all the animals, and after this, when you want a deer to eat, you will have to hunt all over the woods for it, and then maybe not find one. Go home now to your mother, while I see if I can find something to eat for supper.'

When the boys reached home again they were very tired and hungry, and asked their mother for something to eat.

'There is no meat,' said Selu, 'but wait a little while, and I will get you something.'

So she took a basket and started out to the provision-house. This provision house was built upon poles high up from the ground, to keep it out of the reach of animals, and had a ladder to climb up by, and one door, but no other opening.

Every day, when Selu got ready to cook the dinner, she would go out to the provision house with a basket, and bring it back full of corn and beans. The boys had never been inside the provision house, and wondered where all the corn and beans could come from, as the house was not a very large one; so, as soon as Selu went out of the door, the wild boy said to his brother,

'Let's go and see what she does.'

They ran around and climbed up at the back of the provision house, and pulled out a piece of clay from between the logs, so that they could look in. There they saw Selu standing in the middle of the room, with the basket in front of her on the floor.

Leaning over the basket, she rubbed her stomach – so – and the basket was half-full of corn. Then she rubbed under her armpits – so – and the basket was full to the top with beans.

The brothers looked at each other, and said,

'This will never do; our mother is a witch. If we eat any of that it will poison us. We must kill her.'

When the boys came back into the house, Selu knew their thoughts before they spoke.

'So you are going to kill me!' said Selu.

'Yes,' said the boys; 'you are a witch.'

'Well,' said their mother, 'when you have killed me, clear a large piece of ground in front of the house, and drag my body seven times around the circle.

'Then drag me seven times over the ground inside the circle, and stay up all night and watch, and in the morning you will have plenty of corn.'

Then the boys killed her with their clubs, and cut off her head, and put it up on the roof of the house, and told it to look for her husband. Then they set to work to clear the ground in front of the house, but, instead of clearing the whole piece, they cleared only seven little spots.

This is the reason why corn now grows only in a few places instead of over the whole world. Then they dragged the body of Selu around the circles, and wherever her blood fell on the ground the corn sprang up. But, instead of dragging her body seven times across the ground, they did this only twice, which is the reason why the Indians still work their crop but twice. The two brothers sat up and watched their corn all night, and in the morning it was fully grown and ripe.

When Kanati came home at last, he looked around, but could not see Selu anywhere, so he asked the boys where their mother was.

'She was a witch, and we killed her,' said the boys; 'there is her head up there on top of the house.' When Kanati saw his wife's head on the roof he was very angry, and said, 'I won't stay with you any longer. I am going to the Wolf people.'

So he started off, but, before he had gone far, the wild boy changed himself again to a tuft of down, which fell on Kanati's shoulder.

When Kanati reached the settlement of the Wolf people, they were holding a council in the townhouse. He went in and sat down, with the tuft of bird's down on his shoulder.

When the Wolf chief asked him his business, he said,

'I have two bad boys at home, and I want you to go in seven days from now and play against them.'

Kanati spoke as though he wanted them to play a game of ball, but the wolves knew that he meant for them to come and kill the two boys. The wolves promised to go. Then the bird's down blew off from Kanati's shoulder, and the smoke carried it up through the hole in the roof of the townhouse.

When it came down on the ground outside, the wild boy took his right shape again, and went home and told his brother all that he had heard in the townhouse. When Kanati left the Wolf people, he did not return home, but went on farther.

The boys then began to get ready for the wolves, and the wild boy – the magician – told his brother what to do. They ran around the house in a wide circle until they had made a trail all around it, excepting on the side from which the wolves would come, where they left a small open space. Then they made four large bundles of arrows, and placed them at four different points on the outside of the circle, after which they hid themselves in the woods and waited for the wolves.

On the appointed day a whole army of wolves came and surrounded the house, to kill the boys. The wolves did not notice the trail around the house, because they came in where the boys had left the opening, but the moment they were inside the circle the trail changed to a high fence, and shut them in.

Then the boys on the outside took their arrows and began shooting them down, and, as the wolves could not jump over the fence, they were all killed excepting a few, which escaped through the opening into a great swamp close by. Then the boys ran around the swamp, and a circle of fire sprang up in their tracks, and set fire to the grass and bushes, and burned up nearly all the other wolves. Only two or three got away, and these were all the wolves which were left in the whole world.

Soon afterwards some strangers from a distance, who heard that the brothers had a wonderful grain from which they made bread, came to ask for some; for none but Selu and her family had ever known corn before.

The boys gave them seven grains of corn, which they told them to plant the next night on their way home, sitting up all night to watch the corn, which would have seven ripe ears in the morning. These they were to plant the next night, and watch in the same way; and so on every night until they reached home, when they would have corn enough to supply the whole people. The strangers lived seven days' journey away.

They took the seven grains of corn, and started home again. That night they planted the seven grains, and watched all through the darkness until morning, when they saw seven tall stalks, each stalk bearing a ripened ear. They gathered the ears with gladness, and went on their way.

The next night they planted all their corn, and guarded it with wakeful care until daybreak, when they found an abundant increase. But the way was long and the sun was hot, and the people grew tired. On the last night before reaching home they fell asleep, and in the morning the corn they had planted had not even sprouted. They brought with them to their settlement what corn they had left, and planted it, and with care and attention were able to raise a crop.

But ever since the corn must be watched and tended through half the year, which before would grow and ripen in a night.

As Kanati did not return, the boys at last concluded to go and see if they could find him. The wild boy got a wheel and rolled it toward the direction where it is always night. In a little while the wheel came rolling back, and the boys knew their father was not there. Then the wild boy rolled it to the south and to the north, and each time the wheel came back to him, and they knew their father was not there. Then he rolled it toward the Sun Land, and it did not return.

'Our father is there,' said the wild boy, 'let us go and find him.'

So the two brothers set off toward the east, and after travelling a long time they came upon Kanati, walking along, with a little dog by his side.

'You bad boys,' said their father, 'have you come here?'

'Yes,' they answered; 'we always accomplish what we start out to do, we are men!'

'This dog overtook me four days ago,' then said Kanati; but the boys knew that the dog was the wheel which they had sent after him to find him.

'Well,' said Kanati, 'as you have found me, we may as well travel together, but I will take the lead.'

Soon they came to a swamp, and Kanati told them there was a dangerous thing there, and they must keep away from it. Then he went on ahead, but as soon as he was out of sight the wild boy said to his brother,

'Come and let us see what is in the swamp.'

They went in together, and in the middle of the swamp they found a large panther, asleep. The wild boy got out an arrow, and shot the panther in the side of the head. The panther turned his head, and the other boy shot him on that side. He turned his head away again, and the two brothers shot together. But the panther was not hurt by the arrows, and paid no more attention to the boys. They came out of the swamp, and soon overtook Kanati, waiting for them.

'Did you find it?' asked Kanati.

'Yes,' said the boys, 'we found it, but it never hurt us. We are men.'

Kanati was surprised, but said nothing, and they went on again.

After a while Kanati turned to them, and said,

'Now you must be careful. We are coming to a tribe called the 'Cookers' [that is, Cannibals], and if they get you they will put you in a pot and feast on you.'

Then he went on ahead. Soon the boys came to a tree which had been struck by lightning, and the wild boy directed his brother to gather some of the splinters from the tree, and told him what to do with them.

In a little while they came to the settlement of the cannibals, who, as soon as they saw the boys, came running out, crying, and 'Good! Here are two nice, fat strangers. Now we'll have a grand feast!' They caught the boys and dragged them into the townhouse, and sent word to all the people of the settlement to come to the feast.

They made up a great fire, filled a large pot with water and set it to boiling, and then seized the wild boy and threw him into the pot, and put the lid on it. His brother was not frightened in the least, and made no attempt to escape, but quietly knelt down and began putting the splinters into the fire, as if to make it burn better.

When the cannibals thought the meat was about ready, they lifted the lid from the pot, and that instant a blinding light filled the townhouse, and the lightning began to dart from one side to the other, beating down the cannibals until not one of them was left alive. Then the lightning went up through the smoke hole and the next moment there were the two boys standing outside the totownhouses though nothing had happened. They went on, and soon met Kanati, who seemed much surprised to see them, and said,

'What! Are you here again?'

'Oh, yes, we never give up. We are great men!'

'What did the cannibals do to you?'

'We met them, and they brought us to their townhouse, but they never hurt us.'

Kanati said nothing more, and they went on. Kanati soon got out of sight of the boys, but they kept on until they came to the end of the world, where the sun comes out. The sky was just coming down when they got there, but they waited until it went up again, and then they went through and climbed up on the other side.

There they found Kanati and Selu sitting together.

The old folks received them kindly, and were glad to see them, and told them they might stay there a while, but then they must go to live where the sun goes down. The boys stayed with their parents seven days, and then went on toward the sunset land, where they are still living.

From: Myths of the Cherokees

The Wicked Stepmother

ONCE UPON A time there was a hunter, who was a widower and had a son from his former wife. He married another wife, but soon was mortally sick. On his deathbed, he said to his new wife,

'Wife, I am dying, and I know that when my son grows up he will follow my profession. Take care, do not let him go to the Black Mountains to hunt.'

After the death of the hunter, the son growing up began to follow his father's profession and became a hunter. One day his stepmother said,

'Son, your father, when dying, said that after you grow up, if you follow his profession, you should not go to the Black Mountains to hunt.'

But the lad, paying no attention to what his father had advised him, one day took his bow and arrow, mounted his horse, and hastened to the Black Mountains to hunt. So soon as he reached there, Lo! A giant made his appearance on the back of his horse of lightning, and exclaimed,

'How now? Have you never heard my name, that you have dared to come and hunt on my ground?'

And he threw three terrible maces at the lad, who very cleverly avoided them, hiding himself under the belly of his horse.

Now it was his turn: he drew his bow and arrow, took aim, and shot the giant, who was nailed to the ground. He at once mounted the giant's horse of lightning, who, galloping, soon brought him to a magnificent palace, gilded all over with gold and decorated with precious jewels.

Lo! A maiden as beautiful as the sun appeared in the window, saying,

'Human being, the snake upon its belly and the bird with its wings could not come here; how could you venture to come?'

'Your love brought me hither, fair creature,' answered the lad, who had already fallen in love with the charming maiden.

'But the giant will come and tear you into pieces,' said the maiden, who also had fallen in love with the lad.

'I have killed him, and there lies his carcass!' answered the lad.

The door of the palace was opened, and the lad was received by the maiden, who told him that she was the daughter of a prince, and that the giant had stolen her and kept her in that palace, where she had forty beautiful handmaids serving her.

'And as you have killed the giant,' she added, 'I, who am a virgin, shall be your wife, and all these maidens will serve us.'

And they accepted one another as husband and wife.

Opening the treasures of the giant, they found innumerable jewels, gold, silver, and all kinds of wealth. The lad thought such a magnificent palace, with so many treasures worthy of a prince, and the most beautiful wife in the world, were things that he could hardly have dreamed of, and he decided to live there, going to hunt every day as usual.

One day, however, he came home sighing,

'Ah! Alas, alas!'

'How now? What is the matter?' said the beautiful bride. 'Am I and my forty handmaids not enough to please you? Why did you sigh?'

'You are sweet, my love,' said the lad; 'but my mother also is sweet. You have your place in my heart, but my mother also has her place. I remembered her; therefore I sighed.'

'Well,' said the young bride, 'take a horseload of gold to your mother; let her live in abundance and be happy.'

'No,' said the lad; 'let me go and bring her here.'

'Very well, go then,' said the young bride.

The lad went to his stepmother, and, telling her all what he had done, brought her to the palace of the Black Mountains. Here she was the mother-in-law of the fair bride, and therefore the superior of the whole palace. Both the bride and the maidens had to submit to her.

The lad used to go out for hunting. The stepmother, being well versed in witchcraft and medicine, went secretly and administered some remedy to the corpse of the giant, so that he was soon healed. Falling in love with the giant, she took him to the palace and hid him in a cellar, where secretly she paid him daily visits, as she was afraid of her stepson.

Wishing, however, to make her coquetry freely, the witch one day said to the giant,

'Giant, you must advise me a way where I may send my son on an errand, and from where he may never come back.'

Upon the advice of the giant she entered her room, and, putting under her bed pieces of very thin and dry Oriental bread, lay down upon the bed and pretended sickness. In the evening the lad returned from hunting, and, hearing that his stepmother was ill, hastened to her side and asked,

'What is the matter, mother?'

'O son!' exclaimed the witch, with a sickly voice, 'I am very sick; I shall die!' and, as she turned from one side to the other, the dry bread began to crackle.

'Hark,' exclaimed the witch, how my bones are cracking!'

'What is the remedy, mother? What can I do for you?' asked the lad.

'O my son,' said the witch, 'there is only one remedy for my sickness, and that is the Melon of Life. I shall never be healed if I do not eat one of that fruit which you could bring for me.'

'All right, Mother,' said the lad; 'I will fetch you the Melon of Life.'

He at once started on the expedition, and, after a long journey, was guest in the house of an old woman, who inquired where he was going.

When she heard of the errand she said to the lad,

'Son, you are deceived; the expedition is a fatal one; do not go.'

But, as the lad insisted, the old woman said,

'Well, then, let me advise you: on your way you will soon meet with a mansion which is the abode of forty giants, who in daytime go out hunting. But you will find their mother kneading dough. If you are agile enough to run and suck the nipples of the open breast of that giantess without being seen by her, you are safe; else she will make a mouthful of you and devour you.'

The lad went, and found as foretold by the old woman. He was clever enough to suck the nipples of the giantess without being seen by her.

'A plague on her who advised you!' exclaimed the angry giantess, 'else I would make a good morsel of you. But now, having sucked of my breast, you are like one of my own sons. Let me hide you in a box, lest the forty giants should come in the evening, and, finding you here, devour you.'

And she shut the lad in a box.

In the evening the forty giants came, and, smelling a human being, said,

'O mother! All the year long we hunt beasts and fowls, which we bring home to eat together; and now we smell a human being, whom no doubt you have devoured today. Have you not preserved for us at least a few bones which we might chew?'

'It is you,' answered the dame, 'that are coming from mountains and plains, where no doubt you have found human beings, and the smell comes out of your own mouths. I have eaten no human being.'

'No, Mother, you have,' exclaimed the giants.

'How if my nephew, the son of my human sister, has come here to pay me a visit?' answered the giantess.

'O mother!' exclaimed the giants, 'show us our human cousin; we will not hurt him, but talk with him.'

The giantess took the lad out of the box, and brought him to the giants, who were very much pleased to see a human being so small, but so beautiful and manly. Holding him up like a toy, the giants handed him to one another to gratify their curiosity by looking at him.

'Mother, what has our cousin come for?' inquired the giants.

'He has come,' answered the giantess, 'to pick a Melon of Life, and carry to his mother, who is sick. You must go and get the Melon of Life for him.'

'Not we!' exclaimed the forty giants; 'It is above our ability.'

The youngest of the forty brothers, however, who was lame, said to the lad 'Cousin, I will go with you and get the Melon of Life for you. You must only take with you a jug, a comb, and a razor.'

On the following day the lad took what was necessary and followed the lame giant, who soon brought him to the garden of the Melon of Life, which was guarded by fifty giants. The guards being asleep, the lad and his companion entered the garden without being perceived, and, picking the melon, began to run.

But they were just crossing the hedges when the lame leg of the giant was caught by the fence, and, in his haste to release it, he shook the hedges, which crackled like thunder; and, lo! all the fifty giants awoke, crying,

'Thieves! Human beings! A good prey for us!' and began to pursue the lad and his lame companion.

'Throw the jug behind you, cousin!' exclaimed the lame giant.

The lad did so, and, Lo! Plains and mountains behind them were covered by an immense sea, which the fifty giants had to cross in order to reach them. By this means they gained quite a distance till the fifty crossed the sea.

'Now, cousin, throw the comb behind you!' exclaimed the giant.

The lad did so, and, to an extensive jungle between them and the fifty giants. They gained another great distance before the giants finished crossing the jungle.

'Throw the razor now, cousin!' exclaimed the giant.

The lad did so, and, to all the country between them and the fifty was covered with pieces of glass sharp like razors. Before the fifty could cross the distance, the thirty-nine giants came to the rescue of the two and took them safely to their borders.

The lad took leave of his adopted aunt and cousins, and, taking the Melon of Life with him, returned home. On his way, however, he was again the guest of the old woman, who, seeing him come safely, asked if he had succeeded in bringing the precious fruit.

'Yes, I have brought it, auntie,' answered the lad, and told her his tale.

In the middle of the night, when the lad was sound asleep, the old woman got out the Melon of Life from the lad's saddlebags and put a common melon in its place.

In the morning, the lad brought the melon to his stepmother, who ate it and exclaimed,

'Oh, happy! I am healed!'

The lad once more hunts, while the witch and the giant devise new methods to destroy him. This time it is the milk of the Fairy Lioness which is to be obtained.

As before, the youth proceeds on the expedition and becomes the guest of the old woman, who at first dissuades him, but finally gives him advice. He is to shoot the lioness in the forehead. This action will perform the part of a surgical operation by relieving the beast from a pustule, and the gratitude of the animal will thus be secured.

The lad obtains the milk, but steals the cubs of the lioness and is pursued. He is saved by his clever response to her censure. He had wanted the cubs as a keepsake. The milk is presented, but the witch replaces it with goat's milk.

The stepmother blames the giant, whom she had asked to send the youth on a journey whence he would never return, and the giant advises that the youth be asked to procure the Water of Life.

The stepmother again pretends sickness, and asks the help of the hero to seek the Water of Life. The lad mounts his horse and takes with him the two cubs, which by this time have grown into young lions.

As in previous journeys, he comes to his hostess, who warns him,

'This is the most dangerous expedition that every human being has undertaken, and no one has ever returned from the way you intend to go. Be advised, go back; your mother is surely false.'

'Let come what may, I will go,' said the lad, and, taking the two lions with him, started for the fountain of the Water of Life.

He came to the fountain and found the water oozing in with the thickness of a hair. As soon as he placed his jug under it, a sound sleep overpowered his senses, and he remained there benumbed for seven days and nights. Soon innumerable large scorpions began to attack the sleeping hero, but the lions destroyed all of them. Then thousands of terrible serpents made their appearance and assaulted the lad, hissing with their forked tongues. The lions, after a bloody fight, destroyed them also. Soon a whole army of voracious beasts surrounded the fountain in search of the lad. The lions, after a sanguinary strife, succeeded in destroying them also.

At the end of the seven days and nights the lad awoke, and to his great horror saw that he was surrounded by a high wall, which the lions had built of the carcasses of the beasts and serpents they had killed. The two faithful guards were now sitting at both sides of their master and watching his every motion. The lad, seeing them stained with blood from head to foot, understood how much he owed them for the preservation of his life. He then washed them clean with the Water of Life, and taking the jug, which by that time was filled, went to his hostess.

'Did you bring the Water of Life?' asked the old dame.

'Yes, auntie, I did,' answered the lad, presenting her the jug full of water.

'It was not you that succeeded,' returned the old woman, 'but Heaven and your faithful lions preserved your life.'

During the night, as the lad was sleeping, the old woman poured the Water of Life in another vase, and filled the jug with common water, which the lad in the morning took to his stepmother, who, drinking it, said,

'Oh, happy! I am healed!'

The following day the lad again went hunting.

The witch said to the giant,

'Can you not devise some means to destroy my stepson? By Heaven, I will destroy you this time if you do not advise me how to destroy him.'

'Your stepson is brave,' answered the giant; 'he is a unique hero, and no one can kill him but yourself.'

'How? How?' exclaimed the witch with great joy; 'tell me and I will do it.'

'Do you not remember the three red hairs among his black hairs on his head? So soon as they are picked, your son dies.'

On the following day the witch said to the lad,

'Come, son, lay your head in my lap and take a nap.'

The lad did so and soon slept. The witch immediately took hold of the three red hairs and picked them out. A spasm or two, and the hero died.

'Now, giant,' said the witch, 'take that sword and chop this corpse into small pieces.'

'Not I,' answered the giant; 'my hand will not rise to chop such a hero.'

'You coward!' exclaimed the witch, and, taking the sword herself, chopped the corpse into small pieces, put these in a sack, and threw them over the garden wall. One of the little fingers, however, fell in the garden.

The lions apprehended that their master was killed, and his chopped body was in the bag. They immediately took hold of the bag and carried it to the old woman, the hostess of the hero. Opening the bag, she got out the body, and, putting every part to its proper place, made a whole; only the little finger was missing.

She explained to the lions what was missing, and they at once went, and, smelling their master's finger in the garden, found and brought it to the old woman, who put it in its place. Now she brought the Milk of the Fairy Lioness, which she had secretly preserved, and poured it over the body. Immediately all the broken bones, muscles, and sinews came together, and, the members being united, the body became as sound and delicate as that of a newborn babe.

Then she brought the Melon of Life and put it before his nostrils. So soon as the lad smelled it, he sneezed seven times. Then she poured the Water of Life down his throat. At once the lad opened his eyes and jumped up saying,

'Oh, what a sound sleep was this that overpowered my senses!'

'Sleep!' exclaimed the kind woman. 'Yes, a sleep out of which you would have never awaked had not Providence preserved you.'

And she told him what had happened.

'Now, my good hostess,' said the lad, 'you have done me a kindness next to God, a kindness that I can never reward. May Heaven reward you!'

He brought her from his treasures a horseload of gold and a horseload of silver, saying,

'These are for you; spend as much as you like and pray for me so long as you live.'

The lad came to his palace and found that his beautiful bride was imprisoned in a dark cellar, where she was left to starve; while the witch, his stepmother, was in excess of merriment with the giant and half a dozen younglings around her.

They were all horror-struck to see the hero enter it, and the giant was about to make his exit from a secret door in the wall, when the lad seized hold of him, saying,

'How now, coward? Are you running? Stop and solve me this puzzle: who are those ugly younglings that are infecting the very air of my palace?'

'They are my children out of yonder woman, your mother,' answered the giant.

'Mother? I have no mother!' exclaimed the lad. 'You increase so soon, do you? Now we are going to have a great merriment. Go and bring me from the yonder mountain wood enough to build a large pile.'

The giant obeyed, and soon a large pile of wood was built in the courtyard of the palace. The lad struck a flint and lighted the wood. Soon the whole pile was on fire burning like a furnace.

'Now, giant,' said the lad, 'take hold of these bastards, and throw them into the fire one by one.'

The giant obeyed, and all the younglings were burned on the pile.

'Bring now yonder witch, and throw her into the fire!' ordered the lad.

She also shared the fate of her bastard children.

'Now shall I throw you also?' asked the lad of the giant.

'Hero!' exclaimed the giant, 'I honour you; I will obey you.'

'Well, then,' said the lad, 'I will not kill you. Come, pass under my sword and swear obedience to me.'

The giant kissed the sword, and, passing under it, became the bondman of the lad.

The lad then released his beautiful bride from her dark prison. They celebrated anew their nuptials for forty days and forty nights, and enjoyed a happy life thereafter.

Thus they attained their wishes. May Heaven grant that you may attain your wishes!

Three apples fell from heaven: one for me, one for the storyteller, and one for him who entertained the company.

From: The Wicked Stepmother

The Tale of Suto & Tato

Suto is Agha of the Duskani tribe, from the village of Horamar and of the clan of Mala Miri. Tato is Agha of the Rekani tribe, of the village of Razga, and the clan of Mala Mikail Agha.

The Rekani, from early times till now, have been continuously under the hands of the Horamar Aghas, and in the time of Suto Agha they fell even more completely under their dominance.

Suto, with his sons, his brothers, and the elders of his clan visited many persecutions and impositions upon the Rekani, and rendered them so desperate that the power of forbearance no longer remained to them.

Tato, yet a youth, was a man of much courage, the like of whom had never been seen among the Rekani Aghas, and now his pride could no longer brook the misrule of the Horamari. He said to his brothers, Temo, Hadi, and Resul,

'I cannot submit like you, death is pleasanter than life thus; with God's help I shall terminate Suto's powers whether I die or live.'

His brothers and relations replied,

'We shall run counter to any plan you may consider advisable; but we shall be annihilated, for we are not strong enough to cope with the Horamari.'

Tato replied,

'And if we be annihilated, there is no loss. If we prevail, we have profited in name and honour till Judgement Day, and if vanquished we die and are at rest. Whatever comes to pass I am resigned.'

So they thus perfected their agreement to a feud with the Horamari.

One day it so happened that Haio, Suto's brother, in accordance with his custom, visited the Rekani villages and commenced harrying and plundering. Tato and Tamo accompanied by ten of their men approached him and said,

'Go out from amongst our people! From this day on we do not consent to your coming or going in Rekani.'

Haio said,

'Nevertheless, we are here, and we do not regard you as of any importance.'

When Haio spoke thus Tato presented his rifle, discharged a cartridge, and killed him on the spot. Some of Haio's followers were also killed, and others got away to Nerva, Suto's village, the distance between Nerva and Razga being less than two hours.

The following day Suto collected all the tribesmen of Duskan and Horamar, and said,

'Now will I go at once and annihilate the clan of Mikail Agha Rekani, and will seize all the Rekani land as revenge for Haio.'

All said,

'We are ready, whatever you order, we shall execute. Certainly the revenge of the Agha's brother is a duty upon all of us, and even without your orders it is incumbent upon us day and night to strive for Haio's revenge.'

So Suto with his force came upon Razga village and opened the fight. Tato's men were few, and could not fight in the open, so took cover in Tato's fort, and from there engaged Suto's forces.

They became surrounded, and Suto's men were pressing the attack. At the portal of the fort Tato was seated at an embrasure over the door and killed four or five at every rush, throwing them back. Suto said,

'This will not do, we must approach the fort with a chirpa [a movable fence, shield or blockade].'

They cut some trees from Razga village, and dismembered them, constructed a chirpa and advanced towards the fort, and about the fourth or fifth hour of the night they got the chirpa up to it, and from its top a few men got upon the roof of the fort, and Tato's men became hard pressed. But Tato said,

'Fear nothing, a man is for such a day as this, to seize, to kill, that is the manly way. Wait, and now will I scatter them.'

He soaked four or five quilts in kerosene, spread them on poles, thrust them in the chirpa, and fired them. The eaves of the fort were all stone, and did not catch fire.

When the flames of the chirpa rose, all sides of the fort were illuminated. Tato and his men fired several volleys upon Suto's force, and in that time finished off twenty-four people. Once again Suto's men were forced back, the chirpa availed not.

He called out to Tato,

'I go to prepare destruction for you, this time I will make a chirpa of stone. Then you cannot fire it.'

Tafo answered him, and called out,

'I have debauched thy father! Your wooden chirpa did not avail, and before you can bring a stone one to the fort a long time will pass. Perhaps by then God will find me some means.'

They commenced the construction of a stone chirpa, but it was not so easy as the wooden one. During this time information reached the Government of Amadia that for the last twelve days Suto had been besieging Tato's fort, and he with his men was beleaguered.

The Qaim Maqam, the governor of Amadia then sent a gendarme officer with twenty gendarmes to Razga to remove Suto's force from the attack on Tato by whatever means possible.

The officer and gendarmes reached Razga and saw a great concourse about it. They reasoned that the affair could not be hurried, it would only be possible with stratagem and cunning. Since many men had come to their death; with but twenty gendarmes fighting, the affair would not be resolved, and to consent to do so, moreover, would be far from sense.

The officer addressed Suto: 'I have come specially to you to say that I do not desire that your clap should be destroyed, as you are a well-born and respectable Agha. It is now several days since, that you have brought your force against the Rekani, and are fighting. The noise of it has reached the province of Mosul, and the wali has informed to Qaim Maqam of Amadia that he has heard such a rumour, and ordered him to make searching inquiries, and if it is correct to let him know quickly, when he will inform the Wali of Van that he may send royal troops from Van against the tribe of Suto. Also from Mosul two battalions with two guns will come to discipline Suto and protect Tato.

'Since things are thus, the saving of your position is, that in one hour you disband your force, when we shall reply to the Wali of Mosul that nothing of importance has occurred, that some men of Suto and Tato had quarrelled behind the village about the matter of some vineyard theft for two or three hours, and had now separated with two or three men wounded. Then you will not be responsible. So, I have told you. Consent, as you like; or dissent, as you like.'

When the officer thus spoke, all the people said to Suto,

'We will not destroy our homes, conflict with the Government is too much for us. If it is tribal warfare we are all ready to give ourselves to killing for you. But against the Government is not possible for us.'

In the end Suto consented, and retired his force.

The officer took much money from him, and also placed a heavy obligation upon him, inasmuch as he had arranged his affairs with ease. He also said to Tato,

'To save your position it is best that you should transport your household and family and your relatives to the headquarters of the Amadia cannon; inform the Vilayet and the Sublime Porte, the Sultan's Court, at Constantinople.

Catalogue your grievances and injuries before the necessary departments, and perhaps the Government may give you its protection. Otherwise you will not be able to defend yourselves against the pressure of the Aghas of Horamar. We also will all bear witness for you.'

In the end he made Tato also acquiescent and grateful, and took all his family and following with him to Amadia. Also he profited by much money from him. For there is a popular proverb amongst the Kurds:

'Turks are vultures, their pleasure is in being full of carrion.'

When Tato with all his people went to Amadia the lands of Rekani were left without a guardian. Sheikh Muhammad Sadiq was also a great vulture, and the Rekani lands were equally a very fat and pleasing carcass.

The avidity of the noble sheikh became most overpowering, and he took thought to himself how he could easily bring the lands of Rekani under his own hand. He sent a confidential letter, by the hand of two or three respectable and intelligent men, together with some money to the Qaim Maqam of Amadia, saying,

'I beg of you to so arrange that Tato should need me, and come here, that I may say to him that will get his business arranged. You on your side, hinder it somewhat.'

When the letter reached the Qaim Maqam it pleased him very much, and he acted in accordance with the sheikh's aims, saying to Tato,

'I have thought of a surer and easier way for you. Although here also your affairs may be arranged, the Mosul Vilayet delays matters, and before a result eventuates one becomes most disgusted. The Van Vilayet puts things in hand more quickly, and in that Vilayet, everything is in the hands of Sheikh Muhammad Sadiq, who does as he likes. I say if you and your brothers and some of the notables of the Rekani tribe go to Neri before Sheikh Muhammad Sadiq, your affairs will be sooner arranged. That both tribally and officially the sheikh be partner and protector is better for you, and then Suto's back will break.'

In fine, he convinced Tato, who was grateful to the Qaim Maqam for showing him such a course. So Tato with his brothers and the notables came to Neri, and the game entered the nets of the sheikh.

When he came before Sheikh Muhammad Sadiq, the latter showed him much honour and graciousness. He was more soft-tongued than a Pawai, and soothed Tato's heart by all means possible. He said,

'Sell me the site of Razga Fort, I will then entirely demolish it and build it again larger and stronger. will place twenty of my own men with you, and will give your men a hundred Martini and Mauser rifles, and will also procure a special order from Government for your protection. And in exchange for this the elders of the Rekani shall give me one-tenth of their harvests each year.'

Tato replied, 'Whatever the sheikh order, I consent.'

In the end their pact was thus resolved, and Tato deceived. Sura Chaush [chaush, sergeant] with twenty chosen men was sent with Tato among the Rekani. They entirely razed Razga fort, and sent masons, who commenced rebuilding it. The lower stories were approaching completion when Suto came to the conclusion that if Razga fort be completed in this style and the sheikh support the Rekani, Tato's strength would reach such a degree that he could no longer oppose him, and in the end there would be great distress for the Agha of Horamar. Also the caravan road from Horamar towards Mosul, Akra, and Amadia passes through the Rekani.

Suto therefore summoned all the Duskani and Horamari, and said to them,

'You all know to what extent Tato Rekani is my enemy.'

They replied,

'Yes, Agha, we know well.'

He said,

'You all know how masterful and rapacious is Sheikh Muhammad Sadiq?'

They replied,

'Yes, Agha.'

He said,

'You know that if the Razga fort be finished upon those foundations and the sheikh combine with Tato, the lands of the Duskani and Horamari will be entrapped, and we shall be forced to submit to Tato, or else not live.'

They all said together,

'Yes, Agha, we know it is thus, and more.'

Suto said to his people,

'Good, since you all confirm this, why do you not plan how to prevent them, for now we are placed between death and life, and death is the nearer. Enough, either you make a plan, and I will fall in with your ideas, or I will think it over, and you will act in accordance with what I say.'

They replied,

'So long as the person of our Agha is present, no one is the possessor of an opinion. Whatever the Agha decide, our duty is obedience.'

Suto said,

'Since you are so submissive, let it be agreed that I sacrifice myself to your saving. First,' he said, 'my people! You know that I did humble myself to Sheikh Muhammad Sadiq enough that I give him one of your villages for him to show gratitude and for my honour to be vastly greater than that of Tato.'

They all said,

'We believe it. It is even as the Agha says.'

Suto said,

'Good, whatever I do is for your sakes, and not for myself. My idea is this. Let us attack Razga and kill Sura Chaush and the sheikh's men, and not allow Razga fort to be completed. How do you think that would do?'

They said:

'We are steadfast in the Agha's opinion, for whenever the Razga fort be finished we shall be destroyed, so that war is the better course for us, when, if we are to be destroyed, it will be with honour and good fame, not with meanness and dishonour.'

So at dawn nine hundred men of the Duski and Horamari attacked Razga. That day Tato and his men had gone to Amadia to fetch their families to Razga, and only Sura Chaush with twenty men was there. The fort was not yet finished. For an hour they fought, and Suto's force surrounded them on all sides. Sura and his men retired to a house, but it was not suitable for defence. Suto's people came right up to the walls of the house, and though from the lattice Sura killed two or three of Suto's men, it was of no avail. They fired the house at every corner, and Sura with twelve men were faced with burning. They fought to the utmost, and did not surrender their arms, but seven men asked for mercy and emerged. Suto said to those seven,

'Give up your arms, and go before the Sheikh himself, and tell him not to think again of the lands of Rekan. So long as a lad of the Mala Miri is left, no one can with impunity trespass upon the clan of the Rekani.'

Those seven servants came to the sheikh stripped, without arms, miserable, shamefaced. Everyone remained aghast, and said,

'What state is this?'

They described their misfortunes in full, and when they had told the tale of their condition to Sheikh Muhammad Sadiq he was enraged to the utmost degree. For two reasons: one was that the wheat and rice of the Rekani had not fallen into his hands, and the other that great loss and dishonour had come to him. The sheikh fell to thoughts of vengeance for this affair. He collected his chief men and consulted with them,

'What course can you see?' he said.

A few replied,

'Let us collect a large force from the tribes and attack and annihilate them all.'

Some said,

'The course is that full details of his actions be laid before the Valis of Van and Mosul, and that through Government he come to judgment, and that by the hand of Government he come to chastisement.'

And others said,

'It is well that the sheikh show favour to Abdurrahim Agha. He is of the Mafi, and between them and the Mala Miri is ever enmity. Then he and Tato would unite, and when enemies thus appeared from outside and inside, he would be hard pressed.'

Others yet said,

'Let us raid their villages and hold up their caravan roads, nor allow them rest till we fully achieve our revenge.'

In short, each one gave some opinion.

I, the humble Mulla [Islamic teacher] Said, was not at the conference, but at the school teaching the students. A servant came and summoned me to the sheikh. I went into his presence and he asked me,

'What do you think is the best method of revenging Sura Chaush and his men?'

I replied,

'I am a mulla and am young; of matters of policy I know nothing. I have not, much, nay, even hardly, mixed in mundane affairs. Here, all present are intelligent, important, and experienced. They necessarily know better than I.'

The sheikh said,

'It is as you say, but I desire that you also give your opinion, whether good or bad, for they have all expounded their own ideas.'

I asked, 'Of all their opinions, which has appeared to your reverence the most acceptable?'

The sheikh replied,

'As yet I am saying nothing till you also say what is your opinion.'

I said,

'I beg that I may know the opinions of the others, and if they agree with mine I will confirm them, and if not in agreement, then to the degree of my defective wits I also will lay some proposal before you.'

The sheikh repeated the opinions of the conference in detail, and said,

'These are they, their ideas, let me see now what you will say.'

I replied,

'The idea of the tribal force without the knowledge or cooperation of Government is bad, headstrong actions are eventually the cause of damage and remorse. Raiding and caravan-plundering also are but the work of brigands. They are not worthy of the honour and repute of a great one like you, the spiritual head of the humble. Friendliness toward Abdurrahim Agha is indeed good, but in that case, when Suto is disposed of, it is unlikely to profit our cause, and even if it do so will take a long time. Representation of his conduct to the Walis and his being brought to justice by Government is certainly necessary, but the first consideration is that possibly so much alone may not be enough and will not cure our ills.

'At most, Government will imprison him and after a time will take a deal of money from him and release him, when he will become still stronger and our affairs yet more deranged. I consider best thus: First, representation of his conduct to Government; next, the procuring of an official order and the stationing of ten gendarmes for the repair of Razga fort, and the testimony of Tato that the village and fort of Razga have been sold by him to sheikh Muhammad Sadiq. Then, that Government give permission to Sheikh Muhammad Sadiq to protect the village and install at Razga his own armed men therefore. Then, whatever incident occurs, no fault is on the sheikh, it is on Suto.

'Very good presents should be sent to the Qaim Maqams of Giaver and Amadia to gratify them, so that they will write well of the sheikh and evil of Suto. Four hundred men, one hundred Shemdinan, one hundred Girdi, one hundred Herki, one hundred Muzuri, who regard themselves as your adherents, should be sent with Tato to Razga while the fort is being finished and the gendarmes and masons are yet on it. Every night the men should attack one Duskani village. Then our revenge will be both tribal and governmental, and the aim of the sheikh, which is to possess the Rekani, will be achieved and all four tribes will become enemies of Suto. And then neither he nor his descendants can ever be at rest from those four tribes.'

When I outlined this plan, the sheikh was so pleased, and laughed so much, that a hen with all its feathers might have flown into his mouth.

He said,

'Bravo! Mulla Said. Your idea pleases my mind better than any other, and I shall work according to your scheme.'

The members of the conference also agreed that my ideas were more practicable and profitable than any others. The sheikh continued,

'And, since your plan is better than all the others, I should like you to take the trouble to go to Razga and be with my people yourself till the castle be finished. Without your consent, no one shall do anything.'

Then I represented that such was not my duty, but the sheikh became more persistent. In the end four hundred men and ten gendarmes were collected, as I had suggested, and were handed over to me.

I petitioned the sheikh to allow Shuhabeddin, his nephew, Mulla Musa, his secretary, and Qatas Agha, his steward, all three, to come as well. The sheikh asked,

'What are they for? They are not necessary when you are there, what need of anyone else?'

I replied,

'A heavy beam needs many backs to sustain it, for a single one would break under it; this is a great undertaking, and very exacting, and if one has to cope with all its demands, confusion will result, and the work suffer. Since Shuhabeddin is your nephew his influence and value are greater; it is necessary that he come as commander of the fighting men. Mulla Musa is necessary for letter writing and advice upon affairs, and Qatas Agha for the men's rations and collection of the harvests. If I have to do all these my reason will become deranged and unable to cope with the real difficulties.'

Once more all the members of the meeting confirmed what I had said.

The sheikh also agreed, and again commended me, and sent us.

At night we arrived at Mazra and Begoz, and the following day reached the gorge of Herki. The next night we went to Deri, and that same night sent fifty selected men to the hill above Peramizi, which is at the boundaries of the Rekani, Herki, and Duskani, because if that hill be taken no one could get to the Rekani. We rose with the dawn and pressed forward for one stage, nor rested till we reached Razga, and when we arrived there but half an hour was left to sunset.

At once I sent one hundred men, twenty-five from each tribe, onto the hillock before Nerva, Suto's village. I gave them instructions that no one should fire a rifle nor attack till morning, when I would come myself. If that night Suto rose and escaped, good; if not, they should surround the village and not allow anyone to emerge. That night Suto's spies were among the Rekani and warned him that this time such a force had come to Razga, both tribal and government, that he can no longer remain at Nerva.

So that night he arose and went to Horamar.

With the dawn those of us who had remained at Razga reached the others who had gone to the hillock before Nerva, and together surrounded and fired a volley on the village, and no sound came from it. By degrees the men sneaked up to it and saw it was deserted and no one in it.

We also went to it, and I said to Tato,

'This time it is your turn, take your revenge, Tato.'

His men set fire to the forts of Nerva, and the whole village burned. It being time of ripening grapes the force went into the vineyards and brought loads of grapes to Razga. The masons resumed work on the fort. The day after, we left one hundred men there, and three hundred with

Ahmed Beg Barasuri (who was one of Sheikh Muhammad Sadiq's chaushes) we sent against Biri and Chi villages. They plundered them thoroughly, and brought back all the sheep and mules to Razga.

I then sent a letter to the sheikh that,

'Thanks to the shadow of the protection of your exalted ancestors, the raiders of the sheikh reached Razga with all ease. One after the other successes and victories, with attainment of all desires, had been won from the enemy, and the details are thus and thus.'

The sheikh was most delighted, and congratulated us upon our victories. He wrote,

'At present my constant hope is in the perfection of understanding and wisdom and courage of such as you. Then those gratifying victories are yet greater – God be with you. Amen. Sadiq.'

Let us resume the tale of Suto's plight.

When he went to Horamar he sent Mulla Hasan Shuki, who was his clerk, and Qazi of Duskan and Horamar, to Tahir Agha Giaveri, and when the latter reached Tahir Agha he said,

'Suto Agha has sent me to you. You are an Asad Aghai, the head of all the Duskani tribe, and you are in touch with government at Giaver. Friendship is for such a day. Now what are we to think? And what are we to do?'

Tahir Agha, a man of experience, said to Mulla Hasan,

'I have to think somewhat. At present for Suto, except to pacify Sheikh Muhammad Sadiq, there is no course left, as his quarrel with Tato and Sheikh Muhammad Sadiq's men, and the killing of Sura Chaush and twelve men, is well known everywhere. The Government is a supporter of the sheikh. Therefore, now it is necessary to pacify the sheikh.'

Mulla Hasan said,

'Yes, it is as you say. I also think the same, but I do not know where lies the way to the pacification of the sheikh.'

Tahir Agha replied,

'It is certainly difficult, but, if it be possible for you to go to Razga to Mulla Said, ask him if it can be done; he may tell you some way.'

Mulla Hasan left Tahir Agha with the intention of coming to me, and arrived at the village of Hishi in Rekani, a Christian village which is an hour distant from Razga, and remained there the night.

In the early morning we saw a Christian man come before me from there who said he wished to see me alone. When he saw me he said,

'Suto's clerk is sitting in my house and says he would much like to come before you and give you his news, but does not dare on account of outposts who might kill him.'

I then sent ten men with the Christian, and said to them,

'Go and bring Mulla Hasan in safety here, if a hair of his head fall, I will make of you all a target for Martinis.'

So the men went and fetched him, and he remained two nights with us, and we discussed everything. I said to him,

'If the sheikh accept Suto and forgive him for the killing, do you promise that he will go before the sheikh?'

He said,

'Yes, but on condition that Suto be certain of his own life.'

I said,

'Good, go to Suto and explain all to him and get his promise, and by the time you return I shall have communicated with the sheikh and obtained his decision.'

We sent Mulla Hasan back to Suto and I commenced correspondence with the sheikh. Since I knew the habit of Turkish officials, how their word and deed were never in agreement, and that except for the cooking of the roast of their own ends they have no care, I knew that in a short time they would again bring Suto to distress, and even take large sums of money from the sheikh, and afterwards, step by step, favour Suto, and in turn take money from him.

They destroy no man for another's sake. I therefore deemed it suitable thus, that the sheikh accept Suto, for as yet he had not lost his grip of affairs. Finally, I wrote to the sheikh in this sense and set forth the details of Mulla Hasan's coming and going and our conversations together, and sent the letter.

The sheikh sent me reply,

'Whatever be the means of protecting my name and honour in these affairs, you are my agent and attorney. In future you need not refer to me. Such as you think right, so do, beloved.'

The day after arrival of that reply, Mulla Hasan returned to Razga and said,

'If you are certain of the sheikh, I am certain of Suto, that he will not disregard my advice.'

I said,

'Since it is so, and we are both agents, I consider Suto's best course thus, to take Tahir Agha and Ali Effendi Pailam with him and go to Neri to the tomb of Savid Taha, when the sheikh may forgive him. If Suto do not thus, you know he is culpable before Government and will come to destruction.'

Mulla Hasan said,

'If you know that it will be well thus, I will do so.'

I reassured him and he departed, and, having spoken to Suto in this sense, the latter consented and went with Tahir Agha and Ali Effendi to Neri. The sheikh was most gratified, for his desire was ever to get fine flour from between two hard millstones. It was not for grief over Sura Chaush: he wanted money. He said to Suto,

'For the sakes of Tahir Agha and Ali Effendi, and for the sake of the honour of my grandfather's grave, I have forgiven you for killing and seizing and exiling. But the orphans of Sura Chaush are poor, and the dependants of his men are helpless. The blood money of each is one hundred liras. Give one thousand three hundred liras, and depart with well-wishing to your own house.'

Suto having agreed, two gendarmes and eight men were handed over to him to go among the Duski and Horamari to collect thirteen hundred liras for the sheikh and bring it. In the end he apportioned more than three thousand among the Duski and Horamari, and collected it. Thirteen hundred was given to the sheikh, and he took the residue for himself.

When Suto thought it over, he realized that if Tato became a sheikh's man, and the sheikh's servants be continuously with Tato, his own condition would become uncertain and his profits diminish, so he said to himself that it would be well to make such plans regarding Tato as to destroy him by pretence of friendship.

After a year, when all the lands of the Rekani had fallen into the Sheikh's hands with their harvests (not a donkey's ear reached Tato), Suto knew that there was a chance to humiliate Tato. He sent Mulla Hasan to him, having told him,

'What is past is past, may he and I make a compact and from now hence become friends, and, as formerly, do one another no harm. Sheikh Muhammad Sadiq is a dragon, and will eventually devour both of us. It is now a year he (Tato) sees what profit has come to him. To the sheikh's servants there is no difference between him and a [common] Kurmanj.

Now that the sheikh destroys us, it is better that we make peace. If he believe not, I will give him my daughter in marriage that he really believe that I wish peace from my heart.'

Mulla Hasan accordingly went to Tato and spoke to him after this fashion. It entirely won him, and he consented. Suto gave him his daughter.

One day Tato, seizing an opportunity, took all their arms from the sheikh's men, and turned them out disarmed. They came to the sheikh, who was extremely chagrined, but to no good, for Suto and Tato were now entirely reconciled, and together went to the Sheikh of Barzan, who was also an enemy of Sheikh Muhammad Sadiq, and became his adherents. Two years passed thus, and Tato was entirely at peace.

Thereafter Sheikh Muhammad Sadiq died, and the Sheikh of Barzan rebelled against the Turkish Government. By degrees Suto's plans were maturing. He knew that there remained now no sanctuary for Tato, and he considered,

'It is well to make him out guilty before Government, so that when no course be left to him I may destroy him.'

He sent to Tato, whom each year used to pay certain money to Government on account of sheep tax, a message saying,

'What necessity is there for this? All the Duskani tribe pay less than half. This year, at the time of sheep count, send the Rekam animals to us till the officials go, then take the herds back.'

Tato did accordingly. Suto secretly advised the Qaim Magam of Amadia that:

'Tato acts in this manner, and however much I admonish him he heeds not, I know not what to do; for fear of Government I do not dare punish him, otherwise for me to punish, him is easier than to swallow a draught of water.'

The Qaim Maqam of Amadia sent Suto a most grateful reply to the effect that he was authorized to punish any person who in any iota practised deception on the Most High Islamic State, and Suto felt secure.

One day he feigned illness, fell into his bed, and sent word to all his friends and relatives that he was near to dying and asking all to come that they be present at his death. Mulla Hasan was seated by his pillow, and with him was reading the Yasin chapter. All his relatives were collected and were weeping for him. Tato, who was his son-in-law, was also sent for to come and bring Suto's daughter with him, for,

'The Agha is at the point of death, in case they should not see one another alive.'

Tato, with his wife and brother Tamo and four or five servants, went to Nerva, Suto's village. When they arrived they saw everyone weeping for the Agha, and the brothers joined in the lamentations. Tato cried:

'Agha! Agha! Lift thine eyes a little! May we all be thy sacrifice! Would that once again you might arise from this sickness even be I not left on this earth.'

Suto raised his eyes a little, sighed, and said,

'Tato, I am dying. Thank God, my men have seen me once more. Death is God's ordinance, and it is the way of all of us.' He continued,

'Usman, Teli, serve Tato well. So! I die. Tata is your elder brother. Fall not out with him, as formerly.'

All said,

'Yes, whatever the Agha orders, we obey with heart and soul.'

That night a separate apartment was given Tato and Tamo. At the time of sleeping Suto called Usman and Teli and now said to them,

'I am well, my idea is thus.'

They departed lightly and took as many men as necessary to the apartment of Tato and Tamo, killed both in their sleep, and disarmed their servants. Suto arose and said,

'Thank God, I have finished my enemy and taken my revenge in safety.'

From: The Tale of Suto and Tato

Ricky of the Tuft

ONCE UPON A time there was a queen who bore a son so ugly and misshapen that for some time it was doubtful if he would have human form at all.

But a fairy who was present at his birth promised that he should have plenty of brains, and added that by virtue of the gift which she had just bestowed upon him he would be able to impart to the person whom he should love best the same degree of intelligence which he possessed himself.

This somewhat consoled the poor queen, who was greatly disappointed at having brought into the world such a hideous brat. And indeed, no sooner did the child begin to speak than his sayings proved to be full of shrewdness, while all that he did was somehow so clever that he charmed everyone.

I forgot to mention that when he was born he had a little tuft of hair upon his head. For this reason he was called Ricky of the Tuft, Ricky being his family name.

Some seven or eight years later the queen of a neighbouring kingdom gave birth to twin daughters. The first one to come into the world was more beautiful than the dawn, and the queen was so overjoyed that it was feared her great excitement might do her some harm. The same fairy who had assisted at the birth of Ricky of the Tuft was present, and in order to moderate the transports of the queen she declared that this little princess would have no sense at all, and would be as stupid as she was beautiful. The queen was deeply mortified, and a moment or two later her chagrin became greater still, for the second daughter proved to be extremely ugly.

'Do not be distressed, Madam,' said the fairy.

'Your daughter shall be recompensed in another way. She shall have so much good sense that her lack of beauty will scarcely be noticed.'

'May Heaven grant it!' said the queen. 'But is there no means by which the elder, who is so beautiful, can be endowed with some intelligence?'

'In the matter of brains I can do nothing for her, Madam,' said the fairy, 'but as regards beauty I can do a great deal. As there is nothing I would not do to please you, I will bestow upon her the power of making beautiful any person who shall greatly please her.'

As the two princesses grew up their perfections increased, and everywhere the beauty of the elder and the wit of the younger were the subject of common talk.

It is equally true that their defects also increased as they became older. The younger grew uglier every minute, and the elder daily became more stupid. Either she answered nothing at all when spoken to, or replied with some idiotic remark. At the same time she was so awkward that she could not set four china vases on the mantelpiece without breaking one of them, nor drink a glass of water without spilling half of it over her clothes.

Now although the elder girl possessed the great advantage which beauty always confers upon youth, she was nevertheless outshone in almost all company by her younger sister. At first everyone gathered around the beauty to see and admire her, but very soon they were all attracted by the graceful and easy conversation of the clever one. In a very short time the elder girl would be left entirely alone, while everybody clustered around her sister.

The elder princess was not so stupid that she was not aware of this, and she would willingly have surrendered all her beauty for half her sister's cleverness. Sometimes she was ready to die of grief for the queen, though a sensible woman, could not refrain from occasionally reproaching her for her stupidity.

The princess had retired one day to a wood to bemoan her misfortune, when she saw approaching her an ugly little man, of very disagreeable appearance, but clad in magnificent attire.

This was the young prince Ricky of the Tuft. He had fallen in love with her portrait, which was everywhere to be seen, and had left his father's kingdom in order to have the pleasure of seeing and talking to her.

Delighted to meet her thus alone, he approached with every mark of respect and politeness. But while he paid her the usual compliments he noticed that she was plunged in melancholy.

'I cannot understand, madam,' he said, 'how anyone with your beauty can be so sad as you appear. I can boast of having seen many fair ladies, and I declare that none of them could compare in beauty with you.'

'It is very kind of you to say so, sir,' answered the princess; and stopped there, at a loss what to say further.

'Beauty,' said Ricky, 'is of such great advantage that everything else can be disregarded; and I do not see that the possessor of it can have anything much to grieve about.'

To this the princess replied,

'I would rather be as plain as you are and have some sense, than be as beautiful as I am and at the same time stupid.'

'Nothing more clearly displays good sense, madam, than a belief that one is not possessed of it. It follows, therefore, that the more one has, the more one fears it to be wanting.'

'I am not sure about that,' said the princess; 'but I know only too well that I am very stupid, and this is the reason of the misery which is nearly killing me.'

'If that is all that troubles you, madam, I can easily put an end to your suffering.'

'How will you manage that?' said the princess.

'I am able, madam,' said Ricky of the Tuft, 'to bestow as much good sense as it is possible to possess on the person whom I love the most. You are that person, and it therefore rests with you to decide whether you will acquire so much intelligence. The only condition is that you shall consent to marry me.'

The princess was dumbfounded, and remained silent.

'I can see,' pursued Ricky, 'that this suggestion perplexes you, and I am not surprised. But I will give you a whole year to make up your mind to it.'

The princess had so little sense, and at the same time desired it so ardently, that she persuaded herself the end of this year would never come. So she accepted the offer which had been made to her. No sooner had she given her word to Ricky that she would marry him within one year from that very day, than she felt a complete change come over her. She found herself able to say all that she wished with the greatest ease, and to say it in an elegant, finished, and natural manner. She at once engaged Ricky in a brilliant and lengthy conversation, holding her own so well that Ricky feared he had given her a larger share of sense than he had retained for himself.

On her return to the palace amazement reigned throughout the court at such a sudden and extraordinary change. Whereas formerly they had been accustomed to hear her give vent to silly, pert remarks, they now heard her express herself sensibly and very wittily. The entire court was overjoyed. The only person not too pleased was the younger sister, for now that she had no longer the advantage over the elder in wit, she seemed nothing but a little fright in comparison.

The king himself often took her advice, and several times held his councils in her apartment.

The news of this change spread abroad, and the princes of the neighbouring kingdoms made many attempts to captivate her. Almost all asked her in marriage. But she found none with enough sense, and so she listened to all without promising herself to any.

At last came one who was so powerful, so rich, so witty, and so handsome, that she could not help being somewhat attracted by him. Her father noticed this, and told her she could make her own choice of a husband. She had only to declare herself. Now the more sense one has, the more difficult it is to make up one's mind in an affair of this kind. After thanking her father, therefore, she asked for a little time to think it over. In order to ponder quietly what she had better do she went to walk in a wood – the very one, as it happened, where she had encountered Ricky of the Tuft.

While she walked, deep in thought, she heard beneath her feet a thudding sound, as though many people were running busily to and fro. Listening more attentively she heard voices.

'Bring me that boiler,' said one; then another,

'Put some wood on that fire!'

At that moment the ground opened, and she saw below what appeared to be a large kitchen full of cooks and scullions, and all the train of attendants which the preparation of a great banquet involves. A gang of some twenty or thirty spit-turners emerged and took up their positions round a very long table in a path in the wood. They all wore their cook's caps on one side, and with their basting implements in their hands they kept time together as they worked, to the lilt of a melodious song.

The princess was astonished by this spectacle, and asked for whom their work was being done.

'For Prince Ricky of the Tuft, madam,' said the foreman of the gang. 'His wedding is tomorrow.'

At this the princess was more surprised than ever. In a flash she remembered that it was a year to the very day since she had promised to marry Prince Ricky of the Tuft, and was taken aback by the recollection. The reason she had forgotten was that when she made the promise she was still without sense, and with the acquisition of that intelligence which the prince had bestowed upon her, all memory of her former stupidities had been blotted out.

She had not gone another thirty paces when Ricky of the Tuft appeared before her, gallant and resplendent, like a prince upon his wedding day.

'As you see, madam,' he said, 'I keep my word to the minute. I do not doubt that you have come to keep yours, and by giving me your hand to make me the happiest of men.'

'I will be frank with you,' replied the princess.

'I have not yet made up my mind on the point, and I am afraid I shall never be able to take the decision you desire.'

'You astonish me, madam,' said Ricky of the Tuft.

'I can well believe it,' said the princess, 'and undoubtedly, if I had to deal with a clown, or a man who lacked good sense, I should feel myself very awkwardly situated.

'A princess must keep her word,' he would say, 'and you must marry me because you promised to! But I am speaking to a man of the world, of the greatest good sense, and I am sure that he will listen to reason. As you are aware, I could not make up my mind to marry you even when I was entirely without sense; how can you expect that today, possessing the intelligence you bestowed on me, which makes me still more difficult to please than formerly, I should take a decision which I could not take then? If you wished so much to marry me, you were very wrong to relieve me of my stupidity, and to let me see more clearly than I did.'

'If a man who lacked good sense,' replied Ricky of the Tuft, 'would be justified, as you have just said, in reproaching you for breaking your word, why do you expect, madam, that I should act differently where the happiness of my whole life is at stake? Is it reasonable that people who have sense should be treated worse than those who have none? Would you maintain that for a moment – you, who so markedly have sense, and desired so ardently to have it? But, pardon me, let us get to the facts. With the exception of my ugliness, is there anything about me which displeases you? Are you dissatisfied with my breeding, my brains, my disposition, or my manners?'

'In no way,' replied the princess. 'I like exceedingly all that you have displayed of the qualities you mention.'

'In that case,' said Ricky of the Tuft, 'happiness will be mine, for it lies in your power to make me the most attractive of men.'

'How can that be done?' asked the princess.

'It will happen of itself,' replied Ricky of the Tuft, 'if you love me well enough to wish that it be so. To remove your doubts, madam, let me tell you that the same fairy who on the day of my birth bestowed upon me the power of endowing with intelligence the woman of my choice, gave to you also the power of endowing with beauty the man whom you should love, and on whom you should wish to confer this favour.'

'If that is so,' said the princess, 'I wish with all my heart that you may become the handsomest and most attractive prince in the world, and I give you without reserve the boon which it is mine to bestow.'

No sooner had the princess uttered these words than Ricky of the Tuft appeared before her eyes as the handsomest, most graceful and attractive man that she had ever set eyes on.

Some people assert that this was not the work of fairy enchantment, but that love alone brought about the transformation.

They say that the princess, as she mused upon her lover's constancy, upon his good sense, and his many admirable qualities of heart and head, grew blind to the deformity of his body and the ugliness of his face; that his humpback seemed no more than was natural in a man who could make the courtliest of bows, and that the dreadful limp which had formerly distressed her now betokened nothing more than a certain diffidence and charming deference of manner. They say further that she found his eyes shine all the brighter for their squint, and that this defect in them was to her but a sign of passionate love; while his great red nose she found naught but martial and heroic.

However that may be, the princess promised to marry him on the spot, provided only that he could obtain the consent of her royal father.

The king knew Ricky of the Tuft to be a prince both wise and witty, and on learning of his daughter's regard for him, he accepted him with pleasure as a son-in-law.

The wedding took place upon the morrow, just as Ricky of the Tuft had foreseen, and in accordance with the arrangements he had long ago put in train.

From: Folktexts: A Library of Folktales

The Unseen Helpers

GANOGWIOEON, A WAR chief of the Seneca, led a party against the Cherokee. When they came near the first town he left his men outside and went in alone. At the first house he found an old woman and her granddaughter. They did not see him, and he went into the sweat lodge and hid himself under some wood.

When darkness came on he heard the old woman say,

'Maybe Ganogwioeon is near; I'll close the door.'

After a while he heard them going to bed. When he thought they were asleep he went into the house. The fire had burned down low, but the girl was still awake and saw him. She was about to scream, when he said,

'I am Ganogwioeon. If you scream, I'll kill you. If you keep quiet, I'll not hurt you.'

They talked together, and he told her that in the morning she must bring the chief's daughter to him. She promised to do it, and told him where he should wait. Just before daylight he left the house.

In the morning the girl went to the chief's house and said to his daughter,

'Let's go out together for wood.'

The chief's daughter got ready and went with her, and when they came to the place where Ganogwioeon was hiding he sprang out and killed her, but did not hurt the other girl. He pulled off the scalp and gave such a loud scalp yell that all the warriors in the town heard it and came running out after him. He shook the scalp at them and then turned and ran. He killed the first one that came up, but when he tried to shoot the next one the bow broke and the Cherokee got him.

They tied him and carried him to the two women of the tribe who had the power to decide what should be done with him. Each of these women had two snakes tattooed on her lips, with their heads opposite each other, in such a way that when she opened her mouth the two snakes opened their mouths also. They decided to burn the soles of his feet until they were blistered, then to put grains of corn under the skin and to chase him with clubs until they had beaten him to death.

They stripped him and burnt his feet. Then they tied a bark rope around his waist, with an old man to hold the other end, and made him run between two lines of people, and with clubs in their hands. When they gave the word to start Ganogwioeon pulled the rope away from the old man and broke through the line and ran until he had left them all out of sight. When night came he crawled into a hollow log. He was naked and unarmed, with his feet in a pitiful condition, and thought he could never get away.

He heard footsteps on the leaves outside and thought his enemies were upon him. The footsteps came up to the log and someone said to another,

'This is our friend.'

Then the stranger said to Ganogwioeon,

'You think you are the same as dead, but it is not so. We will take care of you. Stick out your feet.'

He put out his feet from the log and felt something licking them.

After a while the voice said,

'I think we have licked his feet enough. Now we must crawl inside the log and lie on each side of him to keep him warm.'

They crawled in beside him. In the morning they crawled out and told him to stick out his feet again.

They licked them again and then said to him,

'Now we have done all we can do this time. Go on until you come to the place where you made a bark shelter a long time ago, and under the bark you will find something to help you.'

Ganogwioeon crawled out of the log, but they were gone. His feet were better now and he could walk comfortably. He went on until about noon, when he came to the bark shelter, and under it he found a knife, an awl, and a flint, that his men had hidden there two years before. He took them and started on again.

Toward evening he looked around until he found another hollow tree and crawled into it to sleep. At night he heard the footsteps and voices again. When he put out his feet again, as the strangers told him to do, they licked his feet as before and then crawled in and lay down on each side of him to keep him warm. Still he could not see them. In the morning after they went out they licked his feet again and said to him,

'At noon you will find food.'

Then they went away.

Ganogwioeon crawled out of the tree and went on.

At noon he came to a burning log, and near it was a dead bear, which was still warm, as if it had been killed only a short time before. He skinned the bear and found it very fat. He cut up the meat and roasted as much as he could eat or carry.

While it was roasting he scraped the skin and rubbed rotten wood dust on it to clean it until he was tired. When night came: he lay down to sleep. He heard the steps and the voices again and one said,

'Well, our friend is lying down. He has plenty to eat, and it does not seem as if he is going to die. Let us lick his feet again.'

On finishing, they said to him,

'You need not worry anymore now. You will get home all right.'

Before it was day they left him.

When morning came he put the bearskin around him like a shirt, with the hair outside, and started on again, taking as much of the meat as he could carry. That night his friends came to him again. They said,

'Your feet are well, but you will be cold,' so they lay again on each side of him. Before daylight they left, saying,

'About noon you will find something to wear.'

He went on and about midday he came to two young bears just killed. He skinned them and dressed the skins, then roasted as much meat as he wanted and lay down to sleep. In the morning he made leggings of the skins, took some of the meat, and started on.

His friends came again the next night and told him that in the morning he would come upon something else to wear. As they said, about noon he found two fawns just killed. He turned the skins and made himself a pair of moccasins, then cut some of the meat, and travelled on until evening, when he made a fire and had supper.

That night again he heard the steps and voices, and one said,

'My friend, very soon now you will reach home safely and find your friends all well. Now we will tell you why we have helped you. Whenever you went hunting you always gave the best part of the meat to us and kept only the smallest part for yourself. For that we are thankful and help you. In the morning you will see us and know who we are.'

In the morning when he woke up they were still there – two men as he thought – but after he had said the last words to them and started on, he turned again to look, and one was a white wolf and the other a black wolf.

That day he reached home.

From: Myths of the Cherokee

The Children of the Sun

IN THE LIFE of Manco Capac, who was the first Inca and from whom they began to be called Children of the Sun and to worship the Sun, they had a full account of the deluge. They say that all people and all created things perished in it, in as far as the water rose above all the highest mountains in the world.

No living things survived except a man and a woman, who remained in a box, and when the waters subsided, the wind carried them to Huinaco, which will be over seventy leagues from Cuzco, a little more or less.

The creator of all things commanded them to remain there as Mitimas, and there in Tiahuanaco the creator began to raise up the people and nations that are in that region, making one of each nation of clay and painting the dresses that each one was to wear, those that were to wear their hair, with hair, and those that were to be shorn, with their hair cut; and to each nation was given the language that was to be spoken, and the songs to be sung, and the seeds and food they were to sow.

When the creator had finished painting and making the said nations and figures of clay, he gave life and soul to each one, men as well as women, and ordered that they pass under the earth. Thence each nation came forth up in the places to which he ordered them to go. Thus they say that some came out of caves, others issued from hills, others from fountains, others from the trunks of trees.

From this cause, and owing to having come forth and commenced to multiply, from those places, and to raving had the beginning of their lineage in them, they made huge and places of worship of them in memory of the origin of their lineage which proceeded from theta. Thus each nation uses the dress with which they invest their huacas, and they say that the first that was born from that place were there turned into stones; others say the first of their lineage were turned into falcons, condors, and other animals and birds. Hence the huacas they use and worship are in different shapes.

They say that the Creator was in Tiahuanaco and that there was his chief abode, hence the superb edifices – worthy of admiration, in that place. On these edifices were painted many dresses of Indians, and there were many stones in the shape of men and women who had been changed into those for not obeying the commands of the Creator. They say that it was dark, and that there he made the sun, the moon, and stars, and that he ordered the sun, moon, and stars to go to the Island of Titicaca, which is near at hand, and thence to rise to heaven.

They also declare that when the sun in the form of a man was ascending into heaven, very brilliant, it called to the Incas and to Manco Capac as their chief, and said,

'Thou and thy descendants are to be Lords and are to subjugate many nations. Look upon me as thy father and thou shalt be my children and thou shalt worship me as thy father.'

And with these words it gave to Manco Capac for his insignia and arms the suntur pauear [a feathered staff] and the champi [a mace-like weapon] and the other insignia that are used by the Incas like sceptres. And at that paint the sun and moon and stars were commanded to ascend to heaven and to fix themselves in their place, and they did so.

At the same instant Manco Capac and his brothers and sisters, by command of the Creator, descended under the earth and came out again at the cave of Paccari-Tambo, though they say that other nations also came out of the same cave, at the point where the sun rose on the first day, after the Creator had divided the night from the day.

Thus it was that they were called Children of the Sun, and that the Sun was worshipped and revered as a father.

From: Aboriginal Myths and Traditions Concerning the Island of Titicaca

The Bride From the
Underworld

Ku, ONE OF the most widely known gods of the Pacific Ocean, was thought by the Hawaiians to have dwelt as a mortal for some time on the western side of the island Hawaii. Here he chose a queen by the name of Hina as his wife, and to them were born two children.

When he withdrew from his residence among men he left a son on the uplands of the district of North Kona, and a daughter on the seashore of the same district. The son, Hiku-i-kana-hele (Hiku of the forest), lived with his mother. The daughter, Kewalu, dwelt under the care of guardian chiefs and priests by a temple, the ruined walls of which are standing even to the present day. Here she was carefully protected and perfected in all arts pertaining to the very high chiefs.

Hiku-of-the-Forest was not accustomed to go to the sea. His life was developed among the forests along the western slopes of the great mountains of Hawaii. Here he learned the wisdom of his mother and of the chiefs and priests under whose care he was placed. To him were given many of the supernatural powers of his father. His mother guarded him from the knowledge that he had a sister and kept him from going to the temple by the side of which she had her home.

Hiku was proficient in all the feats of manly strength and skill upon which chiefs of the highest rank prided themselves. None of the chiefs of the inland districts could compare with him in symmetry of form, beauty of countenance, and skill in manly sports.

The young chief noted the sounds of the forest and the rushing winds along the sides of the mountains. Sometimes, like storm voices, he heard from far off the beat of the surf along the coral reef.

One day he heard a noise like the flapping of the wings of many birds. He looked toward the mountain, but no multitude of his feathered friends could be found. Again the same sound awakened his curiosity. He now learned that it came from the distant seashore far below his home on the mountainside.

Hiku-of-the-Forest called his mother and together they listened as again the strange sound from the beach rose along the mountain gulches and was echoed among the cliffs.

'Hiku,' said the mother, 'that is the clapping of the hands of a large number of men and women. The people who live by the sea are very much pleased and are expressing their great delight in some wonderful deed of a great chief.'

Day after day the rejoicing of the people was heard by the young chief. At last he sent a trusty retainer to learn the cause of the tumult. The messenger reported that he had found certain tabu surf waters of the Kona beach and had seen a very high queen who alone played with her surfboard on the incoming waves. Her beauty surpassed that of any other among all the, people, and her skill in riding the surf was wonderful, exceeding that of anyone whom the people had ever seen, therefore the multitude gathered from near and far to watch the marvellous deeds of the beautiful woman. Their pleasure was so great that when they clapped their hands the sound was like the voices of many thunderstorms.

The young chief said he must go down and see this beautiful maiden. The mother knew that this young woman of such great beauty must be Kewalu, the sister of Hiku. She feared that trouble would come to Kewalu if her more powerful brother should find her and take her in marriage, as was the custom among the people. The omens which had been watched concerning the children in their infancy had predicted many serious troubles. But the young man could not be restrained. He was determined to see the wonderful woman.

He sent his people to gather the nuts of the kukui, or candlenut tree, and crush out the oil and prepare it for anointing his body. He had never used a surfboard, but he commanded his servants to prepare the best one that could be made. Down to the seashore Hiku went with his retainers, down to the tabu place of the beautiful Kewalu.

He anointed his body with the kukui oil until it glistened like the polished leaves of trees; then taking his surfboard he went boldly to the tabu surf waters of his sister. The people stood in amazed silence, expecting to see speedy punishment meted out to the daring stranger. But the gods of the sea favoured Hiku.

Hiku had never been to the seaside and had never learned the arts of those who were skilful in the waters. Nevertheless as he entered the water he carried the surfboard more royally than any chief the people had ever known. The sunlight shone in splendour upon his polished body when he stood on the board and rode to the shore on the crests of the highest surf waves, performing wonderful feats by his magic power.

The joy of the multitude was unbounded, and a mighty storm of noise was made by the clapping of their hands. Kewalu and her maidens had left the beach before the coming of Hiku and were resting in their grass houses in a grove of coconut trees near the heiau. When the great noise made by the people aroused her she sent one of her friends to learn the cause of such rejoicing.

When she learned that an exceedingly handsome chief of the highest rank was sporting among her tabu waters she determined to see him.

So, calling her maidens, she went down to the seashore and first saw Hiku on the highest crest of the rolling surf. She decided at once that she had never seen a man so comely, and Hiku, surf-riding to the shore, felt that he had never dreamed of such grace and beauty as marked the maiden who was coming to welcome him.

When Kewalu came near she took the wreath of rare and fragrant flowers which she wore and coming close to him threw it around his shoulders as a token to all the people that she had taken him to be her husband.

Then the joy of the people surpassed all the pleasure of all the days before, for they looked upon the two most beautiful

106

beings they had ever seen and believed that these two would make glad each other's lives.

Thus Hiku married his sister, Kewalu, according to the custom of that time, because she was the only one of all the people equal to him in rank and beauty, and he alone was fitted to stand in her presence.

For a long time they lived together, sometimes sporting among the highest white crests of storm-tossed surf waves, sometimes enjoying the guessing and gambling games in which the Hawaiians of all times have been very expert, sometimes chanting meles and genealogies and telling marvellous stories of sea and forest, and sometimes feasting and resting under the trees surrounding their grass houses.

Hiku at last grew weary of the life by the sea. He wanted the forest on the mountain and the cold, stimulating air of the uplands. But he did not wish to take his sister-wife with him. Perhaps the omens of their childhood had revealed danger to Kewalu if she left her home by the sea. Whenever he tried to steal away from her she would rush to him and cling to him, persuading him to wait for new sports and joys.

One night Hiku rose up very quietly and passed out into the darkness. As he began to climb toward the uplands the leaves of the trees rustled loudly in welcome. The night birds circled around him and hastened him on his way, but Kewalu was awakened. She called for Hiku. Again and again she called, but Hiku had gone. She heard his footsteps as his eager tread shook the ground. She heard the branches breaking as he forced his way through the forests. Then she hastened after him and her plaintive cry was louder and clearer than the voices of the night birds.

'E Hiku, return! E Hiku, return!
O my love, wait for Kewalu!
Hiku goes up the hills;
Very hard is this hill,
O Hiku! O Hiku, my beloved!'

But Hiku by his magic power sent thick fogs and mists around her. She was blinded and chilled, but she heard the crashing of the branches and ferns as Hiku forced his way through them, and she pressed on, still calling,
'E Hiku, beloved, return to Kewalu.'
Then the young chief threw the long flexible vines of the ieie down into the path. They twined around her feet and made her stumble as she tried to follow him. The rain was falling all around her, and the way was very rough and hard. She slipped and fell again and again.
The ancient chant connected with the legend says:
Hiku is climbing up the hill.
Branches and vines are in the way,
And Kewalu is begging him to stop.
Raindrops are walking on the leaves.
The flowers are beaten to the ground.
Hopeless the quest, but Kewalu is calling:
'E Hiku, beloved! Let us go back together.'
Her tears, mingled with the rain, streamed down her cheeks. The storm wet and destroyed the kapa mantle which

she had thrown around her as she hurried from her home after Hiku.

In rags she tried to force her way through the tangled undergrowth of the uplands, but as she crept forward step by step she stumbled and fell again into the cold wet mass of ferns and grasses.

Then the vines crept up around her legs and her arms and held her, but she tore them loose and forced her way upward, still calling. She was bleeding where the rough limbs of the trees had torn her delicate flesh. She was so bruised and sore from the blows of the bending branches that she could scarcely creep along.

At last she could no longer hear the retreating footsteps of Hiku. Then, chilled and desolate and deserted, she gave up in despair and crept back to the village. There she crawled into the grass house where she had been so happy with her brother Hiku, intending to put an end to her life.

The ieie vines held her arms and legs, but she partially disentangled herself and wound them around her head and neck. Soon the tendrils grew tight and slowly but surely choked the beautiful queen to death. This was the first suicide in the records of Hawaiian mythology.

As the body gradually became lifeless the spirit crept upward to the lua-uhane, the door by which it passed out of the body into the spirit world. This 'spirit door' is the little hole in the corner of the eye. Out of it the spirit is thought to creep slowly as the body becomes cold in death. The spirit left the cold body a prisoner to the tangled vines, and slowly and sadly journeyed to Milu, the Underworld home of the ghosts of the departed.

The lust of the forest had taken possession of Hiku. He felt the freedom of the swift birds who had been his companions in many an excursion into the heavily shaded depths of the forest jungles. He plunged with abandon into the whirl and rush of the storm winds which he had called to his aid to check Kewalu. He was drunken with the atmosphere which he had breathed throughout his childhood and young manhood. When he thought of Kewalu he was sure that he had driven her back to her home by the temple, where he could find her when once more he should seek the seashore.

He had only purposed to stay a while on the uplands, and then return to his sister-wife. His father, the god Ku, had been watching him and had also seen the suicide of the beautiful Kewalu. He saw the spirit pass down to the kingdom of Milu, the home of the ghosts. Then he called Hiku and told him how heedless and thoughtless he had been in his treatment of Kewalu, and how in despair she had taken her life, the spirit going to the Underworld.

Hiku, the child of the forest, was overcome with grief. He was ready to do anything to atone for the suffering he had caused Kewalu, and repair the injury.

Ku told him that only by the most daring effort could he hope to regain his loved bride. He could go to the Underworld, meet the ghosts and bring his sister back, but this could only be done at very great risk to himself, for if the ghosts discovered and captured him they would punish him with severest torments and destroy all hope of returning to the Upperworld.

Hiku was determined to search the land of Milu and find his bride and bring her back to his Kona home by the sea. Ku agreed to aid him with the mighty power which he had as a god, nevertheless it was absolutely necessary that Hiku should descend alone and by his own wit and skill secure the ghost of Kewalu.

Hiku prepared a coconut shell full of oil made from decayed kukui nuts. This was very vile and foul-smelling. Then he made a long stout rope of ieie vines.

Ku knew where the door to the Underworld was, through which human beings could go down. This was a hole near the seashore in the valley of Waipio on the eastern coast of the island.

Ku and Hiku went to Waipio, descended the precipitous walls of the valley and found the door to the pit of Milu. Milu was the ruler of the Underworld. Hiku rubbed his body all over with the rancid kukui oil and then gave the ieie vine into the keeping of his father to hold fast while he made his descent into the world of the spirits of the dead. Slowly Ku let the vine down until at last Hiku stood in the strange land of Milu.

No one noticed his coming and so for a little while he watched the ghosts, studying his best method of finding Kewalu. Some of the ghosts were sleeping; some were gambling and playing the same games they had loved so well while living in the Upperworld; others were feasting and visiting around the poi bowl as they had formerly been accustomed to do.

Hiku knew that the strong odour of the rotten oil would be his best protection, for none of the spirits would want to touch him and so would not discover that he was flesh and blood. Therefore he rubbed his body once more thoroughly with the oil and disfigured himself with dirt. As he passed from place to place searching for Kewalu, the ghosts said,

'What a bad-smelling spirit!' So they turned away from him as if he was one of the most unworthy ghosts dwelling in Milu. In the realm of Milu he saw the people in the game of rolling coconut shells to hit a post. Kulioe, one of the spirits, had been playing the kilu and had lost all his property to the daughter of Milu and one of her friends. He saw Hiku and said, 'If you are a skilful man perhaps you should play with these two girls.'

Hiku said,

'I have nothing. I have only come this day and am alone.' Kulioe bet his bones against some of the property he had lost. The first girl threw her cup at the kilu post. Hiku chanted:

'Are you known by Papa and Wakea,

O eyelashes or rays of the sun?

Mine is the cup of kilu.'

Her cup did not touch the kilu post before Hiku. She threw again, but did not touch, while Hiku chanted the same words. They took a new cup, but failed.

Hiku commenced swinging the cup and threw. It glided and twisted around on the floor and struck the post. This counted five and won the first bet. Then he threw the cup numbered twenty, won all the property and gave it back to Kulioe.

At last he found Kewalu, but she was by the side of the high chief, Milu, who had seen the beautiful princess as she came into the Underworld. More glorious was Kewalu than any other of all those of noble blood who had ever descended to Milu. The ghosts had welcomed the spirit of the princess with great rejoicing, and the king had called her at once to the highest place in his court.

She had not been long with the chiefs of Milu before they asked her to sing or chant her mele. The mele was the family song by which any chief made known his rank and the family with which he was connected, whenever he visited chiefs far away from his own home.

Hiku heard the chant and mingled with the multitude of ghosts gathered around the place where the high chiefs were welcoming the spirit of Kewalu. While Hiku and Kewalu had been living together one of their pleasures was composing and learning to intone a chant which no other among either mortals or spirits should know besides themselves. While Kewalu was singing she introduced her part of this chant. Suddenly from among the throng of ghosts arose the sound of a clear voice chanting the response which was known by no other person but Hiku.

Kewalu was overcome by the thought that perhaps Hiku was dead and was now among the ghosts, but did not dare to incur the hatred of King Milu by making himself known; or perhaps Hiku had endured many dangers of the lower world by coming even in human form to find her and therefore must remain concealed. The people around the king, seeing her grief, were not surprised when she threw a mantle around herself and left them to go away alone into the shadows.

She wandered from place to place among the groups of ghosts, looking for Hiku. Sometimes she softly chanted her part of the mele. At last she was again answered and was sure that Hiku was near, but the only one very close was a foul-smelling, dirt-covered ghost from whom she was turning away in despair.

Hiku in a low tone warned her to be very careful and not recognize him, but assured her that he had come in person to rescue her and take her back to her old home where her body was then lying. He told her to wander around and yet to follow him until they came to the ieie vine which he had left hanging from the hole which opened to the Upperworld.

When Hiku came to the place where the vine was hanging he took hold to see if Ku, his father, was still carefully guarding the other end to pull him up when the right signal should be given. Having made himself sure of the aid of the god, he tied the end of the vine into a strong loop and seated himself in it. Then he began to swing back and forth, back and forth, sometimes rising high and sometimes checking himself and resting with his feet on the ground.

Kewalu came near and begged to be allowed to swing, but Hiku would only consent on the condition that she would sit in his lap. The ghosts thought that this would be an excellent arrangement and shouted their approval of the new sport. Then Hiku took the spirit of Kewalu in his strong arms and began to swing slowly back and forth, then more and more rapidly, higher and higher until the people marvelled at the wonderful skill. Meanwhile he gave the signal to Ku to pull them up. Almost imperceptibly the swing receded from the spirit world.

All this time Hiku had been gently and lovingly rubbing the spirit of Kewalu and softly uttering charm after charm so that while they were swaying in the air she was growing smaller and smaller. Even the chiefs of Milu had been attracted to this unusual sport, and had drawn near to watch the wonderful skill of the strange foul-smelling ghost.

Suddenly it dawned upon some of the beholders that the vine was being drawn up to the Upperworld. Then the cry arose,

'He is stealing the woman!'

'He is stealing the woman!'

The Underworld was in a great uproar of noise. Some of the ghosts were leaping as high as they could, others were calling for Hiku to return, and others were uttering charms to cause his downfall. No one could leap high enough to touch Hiku, and the power of all the charms was defeated by the god Ku, who rapidly drew the vine upward.

Hiku succeeded in charming the ghost of Kewalu into the coconut shell which he still carried. Then stopping the opening tight with his fingers so that the spirit could not escape he brought Kewalu back to the land of mortals.

With the aid of Ku the steep precipices surrounding Waipio Valley were quickly scaled and the journey made to the temple by the tabu surf waters of Kona. Here the body of Kewalu had been lying in state. Here the auwe, or mourning chant, of the retinue of the dead princess could be heard from afar.

Hiku passed through the throngs of mourners, carefully guarding his precious coconut until he came to the feet, cold and stiff in death. Kneeling down he placed the small hole in the end of the shell against the tender spot in the bottom of one of the cold feet.

The spirits of the dead must find their way back little by little through the body from the feet to the eyes, from which they must depart when they bid final farewell to the world. To try to send the spirit back into the body by placing it in the lua-uhane, or 'door of the soul,' would be to have it where it had to depart from the body rather than enter it.

Hiku removed his finger from the hole in the coconut and uttered the incantations which would allure the ghost into the body. Little by little the soul of Kewalu came back, and the body grew warm from the feet upward, until at last the eyes opened and the soul looked out upon the blessed life restored to it by the skill and bravery of Hiku.

No more troubles arose to darken the lives of the children of Ku. Whether in the forest or by the sea they made the days pleasant for each other until at the appointed time together they entered the shades of Milu as chief and chiefess who could not be separated. It is said that the generations of their children gave many rulers to the Hawaiians, and that the present royal family, the 'House of Kalakaua,' is the last of the descendants.

From: Hawaiian Legends of Ghosts and Ghost-Gods

The Fifty-one Thieves

THERE WERE ONCE two brothers, Juan and Pedro.

Pedro was rich and was the elder, but Juan was very poor and gained his living by cutting wood. Juan became so poor at last that he was forced to ask alms from his brother, or what was only the same thing, a loan. After much pleading, Pedro gave his brother enough rice for a single meal, but repenting of such generosity, went and took it off the fire, as his brother's wife was cooking it, and carried it home again.

Juan then set out for the woods, thinking he might be able to find a few sticks that he could exchange for something to eat, and went much farther than he was accustomed to go. He came to a road he did not know and followed it for some distance to where it led to a great rocky bluff and there came to an end.

Juan did not know exactly what to think of such an abrupt ending to the roadway, and sat down behind a large rock to meditate. As he sat there a voice within the cliff said,

'Open the door,' and a door in the cliff opened itself. A man richly dressed came out, followed by several others, whom he told that they were going to a town at a considerable distance. He then said,

'Shut the door,' and the door closed itself again.

117

Juan was not sure whether anyone else was inside, but he was no coward and besides he thought he might as well be murdered as starved to death, so when the robbers had ridden away to a safe distance without seeing him, he went boldly up to the cliff and said,

'Open the door.'

The door opened as obediently to him as to the robber, and he went in. He found himself inside a great cavern filled with money, jewels, and rich stuffs of every kind.

Hastily gathering more than enough gold and jewels to make him rich, he went outside, not forgetting to say,

'Close the door,' and went back to his house.

Having hidden all but a little of his new wealth, he wished to change one or two of his gold pieces for silver so that he could buy something to eat. He went to his brother's house to ask him for the favour, but Pedro was not at home, and his wife, who was at least as mean as Pedro, would not change the money.

After a while Pedro came home, and his wife told him that Juan had some money; and Pedro, hoping in turn to gain some advantage, went to Juan's house and asked many questions about the money. Juan told him that he had sold some wood in town and had been paid in gold, but Pedro did not believe him and hid himself under the house to listen.

At night he heard Juan talking to his wife, and found out the place and the password. Immediately taking three horses to carry his spoils, he set out for the robbers' cave.

Once arrived, he went straight to the cliff and said,

'Open the door,' and the door opened immediately.

He went inside and said,

'Close the door,' and the door closed tight.

He gathered together fifteen great bags of money, each all he could lift, and carried them to the door ready to put on the horses. He found all the rich food and wine of the robbers in the cave, and could not resist the temptation to make merry at their expense; so he ate their food and drank their fine wines till he was foolishly drunk.

When he had reached this state, he began to think of returning home. Beating on the door with both hands, he cried out,

'Open, beast. Open, fool. May lightning blast you if you do not open!' and a hundred other foolish things, but never once saying,

'Open the door.'

While he was thus engaged, the robbers returned, and hearing them coming he hid under a great pile of money with only his nose sticking out. The robbers saw that someone had visited the cave in their absence and hunted for the intruder till one of them discovered him trembling under a heap of coin. With a shout they hauled him forth and beat him until his flesh hung in ribbons.

Then they split him into halves and threw the body into the river, and cut his horses into bits, which they threw after him.

When Pedro did not return, his wife became anxious and told Juan where he had gone. Juan stole quietly to the place by night, and recovered the body, carried it home, and had the pieces sewn together by the tailor.

Now the robbers knew that they had been robbed by someone else, and so, when Pedro's body was taken away, the captain went to town to see who had buried the body, and by inquiring, found that Juan had become suddenly rich, and also that it was his brother who had been buried.

So the captain of the robbers went to Juan's house, where he found a ball going on. Juan knew the captain again and that he was asking many questions, so he made the captain welcome and gave him a great deal to eat and drink. One of the servants came in and pretended to admire the captain's sword till he got it into his own hands; and then he began to give an exhibition of fencing, making the sword whirl hither and thither and ending with a wonderful stroke that made the captain's head roll on the floor.

A day or two later, the lieutenant also came to town, and began to make inquiries concerning the captain. He soon found out that the captain had been killed in Juan's house, but Juan now had soldiers on guard at his door, so that it was necessary to use strategy. He went to Juan and asked if he could start a 'tienda,' or wine shop, and Juan, who recognized the lieutenant, said,

'Yes.' Then the lieutenant went away, soon returning with seven great casks, in each of which he had seven men.

These he stored under Juan's house until such time as Juan, being asleep, could be killed with certainty and little danger. When this was done, he went into the house, intending to make Juan drunk and then kill him as Juan had the captain. Juan, however, got the lieutenant drunk first, and soon his head, like the captain's, rolled on the floor.

The soldiers below, like all soldiers, wished to have a drink from the great casks, and so one of them took a borer and bored into one of the casks. As he did so, a voice whispered,

'Is Juan asleep yet?'

The soldier replied,

'Not yet,' and went and told Juan.

The casks by his order were all put into a boat, loaded with stones and chains, and thrown into the sea. So perished the last of the robbers.

Juan, being no longer in fear of the robbers, often went to their cave, and helped himself to everything that he wanted. He finally became a very great and wealthy man.

From: Tagalog Folk-Tales

Finis

Workbooks From The Scheherazade Foundation

We hope that you have enjoyed this collection of stories, gleaned from varying cultural corners of the world, and that you have been entertained by them.

But, have you considered the deeper meanings and interwoven layers that lie hidden beneath the surface?

At The Scheherazade Foundation, we believe that Teaching-Stories contain wisdom, information, and marvels that have the power to transform the way we think, and thereby change our lives.

Employed as a bedrock of culture throughout the centuries – challenging established patterns of thinking, while passing on knowledge and values – tales such as the ones contained in this volume are a rich resource ready and waiting to be mined.

As an aid to help in the perception of less-obvious facets and layers, we have created a series of original Workbooks. Aimed at stimulating thought-provoking discussions and igniting deep reflection, these tools will assist in unlocking the power of Teaching-Stories.

www.ingramcontent.com/pod-product-compliance
Lightning Source LLC
Chambersburg PA
CBHW030234180626
46810CB00008B/3121